THE DREAM COMPASS

Pec-Pec stared at the circle of dolls, hoping for a meaning. His eyes did not move from one to another, but took in all the figures at once, as a whole.

As he stared, a series of shooting stars streaked across his vision until he saw nothing but a mesh of fine tracer lights. The lines then melded together into a pulsing ball of glowing red, rhythmic—bright, then dark, bright again, dark.

When Pec-Pec's vision finally cleared that night, the pulse remained in the form of sound, a throb so low that it was almost beyond human perception. It faded until he could not distinguish it from his heartbeat.

And Pec-Pec had his answer...

THE DREAM COMPASS

JEFF BREDENBERG

AVON BOOKS ◆ NEW YORK

THE DREAM COMPASS is an original publication of Avon Books. This work has never before appeared in book form. This work is a novel. Any similarity to actual persons or events is purely coincidental.

AVON BOOKS
A division of
The Hearst Corporation
105 Madison Avenue
New York, New York 10016

Copyright © 1991 by Jeff Bredenberg
Cover art by Gary Ruddell
Published by arrangement with the author
Library of Congress Catalog Card Number: 90-93198
ISBN: 0-380-75647-1

First Avon Books Printing: January 1991

AVON TRADEMARK REG. U.S. PAT. OFF. AND IN OTHER COUNTRIES, MARCA REGISTRADA, HECHO EN U.S.A.

Printed in the U.S.A.

RA   10   9   8   7   6   5   4   3   2   1

For Stacey

THE DREAM COMPASS

I
A Letter from Camp

Camp Blade, it's mostly mud up here. And trees, too—specially up northwest, where we haven't logged yet. They say we're a few hunnerd miles north of where Toronto used to be, which is why we only get a truckload of women once a year or so. And that's the heart of the catastrophe I'm telling.

This ain't a casual communication. It's a desperate campaign. I've penned three copies so far, and I am concealing each in the usual manner and sending them along Government Supply lines—south, east, and southwest. A printing press would help, I know, but never have I seen one, they're so illegal. Please read and pass along without delay.

If there is oilcloth to spare, or if there is plastic to be found in your Sector, I would appreciate any covering that would protect these pages better than this cardboard and sackcloth. (And if you must eat while reading, please don't dribble onto the pages. You should see the foul stuff I get up here!)

I am thirty-six. Not married, although I tried once this spring, as you will see. The married campmates lodge in

1

*the roomier family barracks, which I had quite looked for-
ward to. They get ten or twelve years there before the
children ship off, maybe even longer if the Lawyer is feeling
charity.*

But I have been skinny to surrender my free time (since
a year ago we get two hours) to the what-all demanded by
marriage and parenting. Free time I read and write. And
the family barracks also are busy places—they say there's
always a grubber in your lap, yours or someone else's—
and only plumb fools get very showsome with reading.
That's the way in Camp Blade anyway, as I'm told it is
most places. I lose the sexual convenience, of course, but
I can spare centimes for the cathouse every few months.
Most of the time I just rub my own bark.

Late an afternoon, it was April 20, one of the Badgers
in the lookout tower rang the ka-oong, ka-oong that signals
an arrival. Most of the loggers had just bused back into
camp, and there already was a fat crowd at the motor port
when the troop carrier rolled in. From the whoops and
hollers I knew, even down at the warehouse, that it was no
wagon of cornmeal. I pulled on jackboots, hauled up the
boardwalk, and splashed into the parking lot, thinking to
be at a sizable disadvantage for being last there. Stupid
feeling really, cause when the matchup starts it's bedlam
anyway, no advantage to anyone.

Except that the Badgers go first. There are a couple-
twelve Badgers here, but just three were interested, and
campmates stood back in a tight circle while they dropped
the tailgate and rolled up the canvas top on the truck bed.
One lady, old overalls and a standard-issue backpack,
jumped the side of the truck and landed in the oil muck on
her hands and knees. She squinted piss anger all around
and slogged through the crowd. Shouted something like, "I
ain't here for this. I'm ticketed to the medical office." Then
she mounted the boardwalk and clumped off alone.

The Badgers—what pig pokers—pranced and paced in
their uniforms, really sucking in the privilege of first pick.
They checked for head lice, held forearms up in the falling
light, mumbled questions that I figured to be severely per-

sonal. They rumined on the answers all somber. Some of the women were polite.

This was that romance promised in the Government announcements. If you gully those fliers read out at assembly, the females trucked up here are of speckless virtue and upbringing. Not even the dullest of campmates believes this. The women are here for the same reasons as men: Most are mandated; a few are idiot adventurers; one or two, like myself, grew up here; and a few are petty criminals working off sentences in privy upkeep or cathouse duty.

The Badgers carried their brides-to-be off in their arms— no ceremony, just to keep them out of mud. The last, Sgt. Krieger, nodded at us and said, "Your turn."

There was a roar like dogfight gamblers. Some of the women laughed; others screamed in true terror. I felt kinda plumby elbowing my way through, but it was the only way, and I had promised myself I'd try. Ta'ang Beecham grabbed the blonde in the flannel shirt and hauled her onto his shoulders. I'd fancied her, too, but Beecham is a head taller. I was pulling over the wall of the truck bed when I came nose to nose with a face of freckles and red hair.

"Let's go," she said, and I answered, "Yeah." Relieved, I tell you, more to have it over than anything; I could get out of this foolishness and maybe, maybe not, get married. I was starting not to care. I'm no prize by face, and this lady was a match for that. A scar separated her left eyebrow, and her nose had been broken enough that it stair-stepped down and ended in a potato.

The first full-figure glimpse I got of Nora Londi came when old gray-head Jim Freeberg grabbed her thigh. She cracked him on the jaw with the back of her right and stood—6-foot-2, 190 pounds, mostly muscle: "I'm spoken for, Pops." Nora shouldered her duffel and we headed for the boardwalk. She moved like a living pile of rocks.

"You don't have to marry me, y'know," I told.

Nora scratched her nose. "You were there at the truck, and we both went for it. That's how it goes. You're gonna back out, ya?"

"No. But it's custom, not law. I checked with the Lawyer. You have a work assignment, right?"

"*Logging.*"

"*Well, you tenny a right to a singles bunk if you want it. Aren't much—a bed with a plywood wall around it and a light hung. It's not often done, understand—by women, I mean.*"

"*I don' mind. Look, I promise not to fall in love, okay?*"

We went on long like that, embarrassing, like two dogs nosing each other's butts. Nora thought about it: "*It's custom, not law. There's a difference, I s'pose, but they don' talk it up much, do they?*" She squeezed my left bicep. "*Logger?*"

"*Supply house. Lifting, uncrating. Move this here, move that there. I can get you anything you want—anything that comes by truck. Hah. Except a woman—we're fresh out.*"

"*I'd like an apple. And tobacco and rolling papers.*"

I pointed out the temporary quarters, six doors down the boardwalk. We kissed—that's what we were supposed to do, right?—and I went back to work. I had never seen a woman that big.

Pages later . . .

My father taught me to read, got me started, least. He disappeared when I was a grubber, like a lot of trouble-makers do—readers, brawlers, jesus folk. Who knows where they go? Prisons? Some say you might disappear to a "*better*" job in a different Sector, which sounds to me a line from another Government flier. Whatever. I don't intend to disappear; sew my eyelids shut, burn the books, or leave them buried—I don't need to read that much.

Ben Tiggle, the warehouse master, is my spiritual father. He is large, dusty, and old, like the warehouse. (The troublous stonework of the warehouse's foundation dates it as a pre-War structure.)

As a tenner I would pry the top off, say, a crate of axe blades. I would wipe the grease-and-straw packing from the steel and mount the blades by number on the storage pegs. An hour in I would find a few pages of scratchings among the axe blades, wrapped in a piece of old raincoat, maybe.

"*Instructions,*" Ben would say, and toss the papers into

a corner. "Just instructions. Damned Engerswedes think we don't know anything." But often there were none of the drawings and arrows and such what come with mechanical instructions, and the text was hand-done, nothing from Government presses. Ben has never fessed to reading, of course. I took it to myself that all brochures, instructions, and writings of any kind ended up on a safe, dry shelf and not in the kindling bucket. I still have those scriptings—buried, of course—decades old, some.

The night I met Nora Londi, minutes before lights out at end of free time, there was a rap at my bunk door. I shoved my book under the mattress and said "Huh?" There are no latches in barracks, but most everyone—except Badgers, of course—follow etiquette. Ben Tiggle entered, rolling his big frame onto the foot of my bed (where else was there to go in these little pigeonholes?). He pulled the door closed. His jowly was grim, spoke in low-tone, knowing how the hiss of whispers carries.

"She's a killer," he said. "I'm sorry, but you must stop this now. She has killed six men, and she don' belong here. Now, she's not my business, but you are. Nuff said."

"Pig shit," I said to him, or something like.

"The Transport driver swears it, and he's the one what carries the passengers' papers. Bimmie at the admitting office talked to him. Londi bitch jumped on at New Chicago, where the Transport officers look the other way for a living—for a favor, maybe."

So when the lights went out I was becoming very distressed about my immediate future.

The page was water damaged and torn. The next intelligible words:

...father, I was told as a child, was the first person to use the term Badgers, I forget myself sometimes. Everyone else has. It started as a word play—people who wear badges, and lowlife critters.

The joke was What has a pointed head, a thick neck, and is low to the ground?

A Badger.

The term is official now, and the door I kicked through,

*while the other campmates lined up for mess hall, read
BHQCB, for Badger Headquarters—Camp Blade. Love was
not the problem. All Nora Londi and I had, at best, was
business: We do this thing together and our lives will be
better. But overnight I had developed a frightsome picture
of Nora: grinning monsterly, flailing a log chain, a spatter
of blood on her work shirt as she lopped off six heads, like
Sampson with his jawbone in the jesus folk's fairy tales.*

Sgt. Krieger was behind the desk, and his eyebrows rose
in that lazy way of Government people.

"They say she's a butcher—Nora Londi. Six men dead,
and I've gotta marry her! You guys brought in a murderer!"
This I shouted at him, and he was not impressed.

Sgt. Krieger snorted, wiped his nose. "Happens every
time we get new blood up here—you know that. Twenty
strangers in camp, twenty sets of rumors flying around. And
a day ain't passed yet." He jerked open a beaten filing
cabinet, flipped down the folders, and pulled one out. He
wiped his nose again and read.

"Damn," he said to me. "She's a killer, all right. Happened just a couple months ago. What do they think this
is—a prison? Guess I oughtta look up my new woman."

I worked through the day at the warehouse. No word.
Ben Tiggle avoided me, staying close to the office. I carted
dried beans and powdered milk to mess hall and helped
with inventory.

Come free time the Lawyer summoned me to his quarters
back of the BHQCB, where the air smells like mold and
never moves. He wore a black suit over longjohns, no shirt.
He's from the Southlands, where it's so hot, they say, the
people shrank. Even at night, the little fellow looked straight
out of bed. He was in his official stance: leaning onto the
lectern at the foot of his bunk, elbows propped at either
side of the Book, which he consulted on all legal matters.
(I have never dared ask to read from it. Talk reading to a
Government man, and the Monitor would hear of it. Then
you disappear.)

He spoke in smoker's voice: "I have ruled your complaint
valid. Nora Londi does not belong in free camp. Your tale
of butcher is exaggerated, course, but that does not change

the legal issue. It seems that, somehow"—*he greased a smile*—*"this Londi woman persuaded a bureaucrat in New Chicago to blur the distinction between prison camp and assignment to free camp. It's unfathomable, I know, but to some imbeciles in New Chicago, the difference is splitting hairs."*

"They can't be sending us murderers! I almost married her," I said.

"Murder?" he said, smirking again. *"More precisely, it was a manslaughter. There was a large brawl, the report says. The only known participant was Nora Londi, identified by a Badger because of her unique stature. And there was a dead man, a drunk with a cracked skull. One . . . dead man."*

"Oh. Maybe she didn't kill him," I said, and I was starting to see the mistake. Ag.

"She was involved. And therefore guilty."

"I withdraw the complaint."

"A fart in the wind!" He fluttered his hands at imagined vapors. *"She doesn't belong in free camp. Besides, she's gone, shipped off in the same carrier she arrived in."*

And we argued on like that and I missed mess call. It did me no good, of course. He had the Book and I didn't. He was the Government and, despite what they say, I wasn't.

So you can see the impossible task, and the help I need from outside. Maps of all Sectors of Merqua would be of great use. And money.

And please locate Nora Londi. Tell her my story. I console myself that anyone might have filed the complaint I did—although none so powerfully as her husband-to-be. I have little practice at emotions, so I am not sure what more to say. Just tell her that I am coming.

2
The Windmill Mountain

"All right, all right. Case number zero-zero-two-three-CB. Twenty-three! What is this place CB that we've had just a twenty-three-history on?" Rosenthal Webb fired out the question in clippy, impatient syllables. He drummed the four finger nubs of his right hand on the polished wood of the conference table.

"Camp Blade."

"Hooo, yes. Camp Blade, by plumb." He should have known, and in a way he did know: The code designations for every Government station, thousands of them, were buried deep in his thought muddle, under the bric-a-brac of twenty years of administrative duties he had performed since his initial training and fieldwork. Now his hair was falling out and his memory was fraying. This didn't feel like a Revolution anymore.

"Sir," ventured Virginia Quale, "Camp Blade is a Northland settlement of approximately—"

Webb clapped his open hand onto the desktop: "A settlement of approximately one thousand—well, maybe fifteen hunnerd by now—people stationed for the purpose of logging and north-post security. It's considered contamination free, relatively speaking, and thus an asset to the gene pool. How am I doing?''

There were seven polite nods around the table. "On the mark, Mr. Webb," said Quale. "We estimate the population well over the old thousand count now, and as for the twenty-three-history, well, from a percentage standpoint, twenty-three cases since we have been keeping records is quite in line with a population that small.''

"And this poor piss-plumb number twenty-three," said Webb, flipping a page of the report in front of him, "is a Mr. Anton Takk, we assume, although his dispatch is unsigned. He's a Supply-houser . . . um-hmmm. A reader, of course, and a writer.'' Webb turned another page as he skimmed. "Apparently considering—and this is months ago—going AWOL. We've got some poor plum-sucker in the frozen north who's taken to the old Supply line communique route.''

Winston Weet interjected from the far end of the table: "He mentions an axe-blade dispatch. It could have been one of mine, for all I know—we quit those sixteen years ago. Some 'em are probably *still* rotting in the warehouses.''

Webb sucked at his lower lip. "In any case," he said, "we have a reader using a discredited form of communication unknowingly. There's at least a fifty-percent chance that he has announced himself to the Government. Hah. If so, maybe the Monitor will promote him—for taking special initiative for self-education.''

"And maybe," responded Quale, "he'll eat him for brekkie.''

"Just how much of this letter can we believe?" asked Weet. His fingers repeatedly fripped across the corner of his copy.

Quale seemed surprised by the question. "How much? Why would he lie? He's taking such a chance with the Government in just what he says that they'd surely send him to Blue Hole. And even if the story were mostly balderdash—this 'pile of rocks' named Nora and all of that— it's obvious that there's a man about to bolt from Camp

Blade without the least bit of outside experience. He *grew up* in a logger camp!''

"I've had a little experience with reworking the truth myself," Weet replied. "But I agree. *Something* is about to happen that we ought to be on top of."

"In any case," Webb said wearily, "I suppose we should try to get to him—preferably before the Government does." There were seven somber nods.

Quale's throat rattled. "My word. A lifetime in this, and we still have not a glint where to find it—the Government, the Monitor." She stared down at Webb's mangled hand. "And don't forget," she told the aging revolutionary, "we are a service organization now. The Lynchburg Doctrine still holds. We *quietly* help the like-minded. Quietly. For this, no bombs. None of those whip traps you buy from that sadist. No one need die. Unless we locate the Monitor himself. . . ."

Webb groaned. "I know I've said this a dozen. But again I have that much, a glint. Not of where he *is*, but how to find him."

Weet sighed. "A new strategy?"

"A new friend."

Quale rapped the edge of the conference table impatiently. "Rosenthal, we can only authorize a quiet, limited mission—to find Anton Takk and offer him aid or hiding among us."

"The Lynchburg Doctrine—" Webb stopped himself. The words had come out too angrily. He breathed deeply and started again. "I consider the Lynchburg Doctrine, as you all know, to be a tragic mistake—we sit here in a hole like a hutch of shivering rabbits. The Monitor found our Lynchburg Station by paid informant, and we can be fairly certain such a massacre will not be repeated here. We are becoming precisely what the Monitor wants—a chess club in hiding."

Virginia Quale raised her right hand. She paused during the silence that the gesture afforded, waiting for diplomatic words to come to her. "The Revolution, as you once fought it, is over. We can't have you tossing hand bombs willy-nilly on the simplest of missions. Let's put it to a vote."

Quale had studied the other faces around the table, and already knew she would win.

Rosenthal Webb pushed through the outer hatch and stepped into a snow-blanketed forest on a mountainside. The white thermasuit and snow boots made him invisible on the landscape. The last daylight had vanished an hour ago. The snow was falling fast and wet, and Webb watched its angle to gauge the wind. The path to the mountaintop had disappeared in the new coverage, but he knew the way well from his nightly ritual.

At the treeless top the visibility was low, but he could still make out the long purple spines of sister mountains all around. He remembered the old name, Blue Ridge. Webb dipped a hand into the snow, felt for the canvas tarp, and pulled it back, baring a thirty-foot panel of camouflaged wood, which was reinforced with steel strapping. He opened the three combination locks, heaved the wood covering aside, and drew out a hand-cranked winch, which he bolted in place on the lip of the box. The handle turned easily, clicking steadily as an eight-bladed windmill, spanning twenty-eight feet, rose above ground. The facing of the blades' brass hub was imprinted with a circle of lettering: CRED FAIGING. Webb stopped once to release the gear lock, allowing the blades to teeter and then pinwheel methodically in the wet night breeze. Deep in the mountain a generator hummed and massive batteries charged.

The whirling blades always revived memories of airplane propellers; Webb had actually seen one of the ancient birds fly once, three or four decades ago, a carnival curiosity patched together by some crackpot on the coastal dunes.

Those were wild days. The Monitor was more a rumor than a ruler, he seemed to remember. A younger could hitch the old highways from New Chicago to the coast on a whim—even take hack from Government trucks if he had centimes to spread around or a bottle to share. But the bunkhouse riots of New Chicago changed all that, and the Monitor's brutal Security force was born. The righteous men and women, who had gleefully flung petrobombs in the streets one day, had gone scrambling for the wilderness the next.

Oh, these benign, rolling mountains had been so welcoming. Such a green and gentle refuge from which to administer a young person's Revolution.

When the windmill was fully extended, Webb rested. This was one of his few remaining physical chores, and he clung to it steadfastly. No, there *was* no more Revolution, just this damned "un-Government" to nurse along, quietly, discreetly, once in a while a clandestine mission to set in motion. "Revolution" meant raiding armories, didn't it? And blowing bridges and stringing up a Badger or two from a lamppost in New Chicago? He regarded the half-fingers of his right hand. He coughed, spat into the snow, and wondered what evil was rumbling down in his lungs. There was no red in the phlegm. Not today, anyway.

Webb turned north. There were four more windmills to set up.

3
A Crossing at River 074

A simple steel device was affixed to the back of Nora Londi's neck with a leather collar, and she thought about it often as she trudged down, down, down. She had not seen it since it had been padlocked there five days before, but she retained an indelible image of its every mean contour. Its spring-loaded power reminded her of a bear trap: Metal muscles were persistently tensed, ready to drive a thick needle into her spinal cord at the flip of a trigger. A snap collar. Tied to that trigger was an ten-foot leather thong, grasped on the other end by the sweat-moist palm of Red Boss.

It was the second day of their descent. Ironically, it seemed to the flatlander Londi, the downhill hike was hard work, every step a braking action to prevent a dangerous, headlong run down the rocky path. Red Boss belched out a *hoof* with every heavy footfall, and each jostle threw the mighty weight of his belly onto his strained canvas-weave belt. His sopping flannel shirt bore the red badge, a horizontal rectangle, of a Sector 4 Transport official. Behind him, the haughty pack llamas followed, murmuring. If

Londi fell, she wondered, would Red Boss let go of the trigger thong? Could he react fast enough? And how sensitive was the trigger?

The vegetation was getting jungly, and insects, horseflies mostly, whirred incessantly. Londi was losing the distinction between her own body odor and the smell of the rich earth. Her brown felt hat, a constant companion for six years, was developing a band of crusty, white salt deposits from her perspiration. Somewhere far below, inviting and invisible through the forest, was the steady, roaring River 074. Londi battled the temptation to ask for a sip from Red Boss's canteen, wary of what brutal form of recreation he might invent during a trailside pause. She badly wanted to wash the taste of Red Boss from her mouth, or at least drown trying. Death was sounding not too bad.

Red Boss had found exquisite pleasure in clamping the collar onto her neck. "You my dawg now, honey," he had said, stroking her hair outside the holding cells of a town, really a rubble field, called Denver. "You my sweet little dawg for the next ten days. You like diggin' with those paws of yours? Good—you gonna be a miner now. I'm gonna take you to your new home. Say 'woof,' honey, say 'woof.' "

Denver was pretty much the edge of civilization, and not a particularly civil one at that. It was populated mostly by salvagers, a dusty and sore-speckled lot who had no qualms about delving through irradiated wastelands for ancient treasures. There were riches to be found in places where the Government would not go. Beyond Denver there was nothing, save a prison-mining outpost somewhere among those black peaks that rose like a curtain along the prairie.

From Denver they had driven southwest as far as the old highways would take them, Red Boss at the wheel of a dilapidated jeep, Londi manacled to the passenger seat. Then the auto's four-wheel-drive came into play on a series of mountain trails, creek beds, and deteriorating macadam roads. Red Boss knew the way well and never consulted a map.

They had abandoned the jeep the day before, and now the sunlight, blocked by the high ridge behind them, began to fail in midafternoon. The steamy air seemed to press at Londi's eyelids, blurring her vision, and fatigue sent her staggering alarmingly often. Once Londi caught a glimpse of shadowy treetops below and thought she saw a human perched in a cliff-clinging spruce. The figure sprouted huge wings and glided into space. An eagle, perhaps. One of the llamas, as if in awe of the sight, gurgled, "Hooooorrh."

That night, Nora Londi's shackle chain was wrapped around the trunk of a long-leafed pine. Her hat lay at her side, tired looking. Insects visited it happily. When Red Boss seemed hypnotized by the camp fire, she pulled at the chain silently and hard, positioning her wrists flat against the steel cuffs to prevent cuts. But the tree bark, it seemed, was the only thing sustaining any damage.

The deadly collar was still in place, the leather trigger thong ending near Red Boss's bedroll. Beyond that the five llamas drowsed, unburdened for a few hours. Still strapped to the largest llama, a 410-pounder named Diego, was a semiautomatic rifle in its leather holster.

"Whadda ya doin'?"

"My evening exercises, Bossman. Isometrics, y'know."

"That chain ain't gonna give, no way, honey. And them cufflocks is solid Masters. I been doin' this too long to get chancerous with prisoners." His red beard ended in a ragged point, which bobbed comically when he spoke. Londi wondered if it had ever caught fire.

"Gotta keep my arm muscles up, ready for that mining, Bossman. Could get flabby just workin' my legs like this."

"Couple more days on the trail, honey, then it's twenty years in a hole—pick swingin', timber haulin'. All the arm work you want. But maybe you'd feel better walking the rest of the way there on all-fours. Hah. Like a dawg!"

Londi leaned back against the pine and closed her eyes. The bark crackled softly against her skull. Her mind wandered to the rowdy, urine-scented streets of New Chicago, then to a guy she had met in some godforsaken Northland logging region—what Sector was that? Anton Takk was the fellow's name, the bastard. Next she imagined a flock of human-size birds circling in the cool dark above the treetops.

"Hey, honey, how 'bout some sportin' before we night out now?" said Red Boss, standing up.

And then Nora Londi thought back, way back, to the boiling summer day she lopped the heads off of six men with a log chain.

The roiling white river was a blinding spectacle when they emerged from the shadows of the forest. For the first time Londi could see both walls of the gorge, towering so improbably high; judging their scale and distance was impossible.

A rotting dory of silver-colored wood was beached nearby, fastened to a rope-and-pulley mechanism set up eons ago for crossing the unruly River 074. The llamas were groaning nervously.

"They don't like the crossing, no sir," Red Boss said, shoving Londi toward the boat. He tethered the llama harnesses to the stern while Londi boarded shakily. "It's not that deep here, really, and llamas keep a better footin' in the riverbed than humans ever could. I only lost two of the buggers to Oh-seven-four in all my years of Transport. Once you're swept away in *this* water . . . downstream . . ." He shrugged and worked his little finger into his right ear. He withdrew the finger and examined the tip. "And if the rocks don't kill you, the Indians will."

"Indians?"

"Cannibals, wild pokers. They'll gnaw yer bones 'n' put yer head on a stake."

"Your mama told you some stretchers, Bossman."

Red Boss shrugged again and tugged on the knot he had made. "All I know is, downstream from here is where I don't go. All you have to show me is one head on a stake to learn that, an' I've seen a dozen."

"The llamas are terrified of the river," Londi said. "Couldn't we ferry them across first—*in* the boat? Couple at a time, maybe?"

"Maybe I should carry the li'l babes in my arms! Waste of time, coddlin' yer work animals. *Quiet,* ya'll. Less go!"

Red Boss shoved off and stood in the center of the dory. Hand over hand, he pulled them into the rushing water. The llamas followed the dory, stepping tentatively into the current, growling and bleating, rolling their brown eyes wildly. The pulley rope quickly lost its slack as the river tugged at the little craft.

Londi studied the boulders downstream. Indians? The river thundered away fairly straight for several hundred yards before disappearing to the right. She planted her booted feet against the bow supports and, as casually as she could manage, leaned back, laying her head at Red Boss's feet.

"Aw," Red Boss drawled, "is the dawggie napping while Bossman works?"

Londi had mentally rehearsed her next move hundreds of times: With a rapid gyration of the forearm, the deadly leather thong was wrapped four times around her wrist, making Red Boss's end of the line powerless.

Red Boss dropped the pulley rope and snorted: "Look, bitch—"

Londi planted a palm against each wall of the dory and pushed. There was a creak as her arm muscles grew bulbous, then a thunderclap of shattering wood. Submerged in a dark storm of bubbles, Londi somersaulted over a stretch of stony river bottom and managed to stabilize her body somewhat in the violent current. The leather thong came freely now: Red Boss had dropped his end. She pictured the mechanism poised at the back of her neck, and wound the thong around her collar to hold the trigger lever flat—and, she hoped, harmless. A thought glinted through her mind: How curious to be underwater and not have breathing your first priority.

She thrust her head up and gasped, sucking in air and foam. Londi gagged, her lungs afire. She tried again and grabbed pure air that time. Slightly downstream she saw a cluster of flailing furry legs. She gasped again. They had rounded the river bend, and the water was churning furiously. She tried to stand, but the current would have none of that.

The riverbanks narrowed to a mere fifty feet, and the pounding current grew ever more violent. The banks were nothing but closely stacked boulders now piled up into narrowing walls, almost like masonry. Then, magically, all was at ease; there was no more clash of rock and foam, no more riverbed at all. Londi, five frantic llamas, and a fat man were airborne, delicately spat off the lip of a monster waterfall.

4
The Dragon Fish

"That's not a real fish!" The challenge came from a smudge-faced six-year-old sitting cross-legged in the dirt among the children down front. This prompted giggles and a dissenting squeal, "It is *too!*" The dozen adults privileged with splintery folding chairs exchanged puzzled expressions: Perhaps it was *not* a real fish.

Pec-Pec was pleased. He preferred audience participation; it provided a chance to improvise, adding a whiff of danger to a magic routine he knew much too well. He thrust his eyebrows up in mock surprise and fanned the fingers of one hand across his eyes, making them glow menacingly red. He blinked, and his pupils again were coal black.

He swaggered to the edge of the tiny makeshift stage and planted his hands on his hips, glaring back at the fishbowl ontop of a pedestal. He crinkled his nose and silently, in exaggeration, mouthed the words, "Not a real fish."

More giggles.

Pec-Pec leaped from the stage and grabbed the doubting six-year-old. Throwing the youngster gently over his shoulder, the magician marched back to the fishbowl. Linny

Bartok howled in glee and terror. His mother, Suz, crossed her khaki-covered legs uncomfortably.

Linny was on his feet again. The magician arched his back and neck down in a stunning act of contortion, like a curious giraffe, touching noses with the grimy tyke. Pec-Pec again mouthed the sarcastic words: "Not a real fish."

Linny stood frozen in his overalls. This dark-skinned stranger before him smelled of mint and coffee. His nostrils flared like the wings of a sea bird, and his chin, oddly, was clean-shaven. Most of his facial hair had been razored away in the fashion of men from the Southlands, except for a narrow, knotty mustache. From the top of his head fell a torrent of black braids, five of which ended in jewel-studded bands of gold.

"I am Pec-Pec, the magic man," came the deep, soft words. "I tell you, that is a fish, a real fish, a dragon fish from the lagoon behind my home far away. Take the fish."

The child examined the fish. Its body measured three inches, with long flimsy fins colored green, red, and gold.

"Take the fish, I say."

Linny touched the bowl, hesitating.

"Not the bowl—the fish. Take the fish." Whispers hissed among the adults.

Linny reached into the bowl. His hand was submerged, but he felt no wetness. The dragon fish surrendered to his grasp and he drew it out. It wriggled a little in the night air, and its iridescent fins wafted lazily, as if they were still aloft in water.

"Is it a fish?" asked Pec-Pec.

"It's a fish."

"Tell me: Is it a *real* fish?"

"It's a real fish," the child squeaked.

"Put it on my tongue, little boy." A long, red V-shape snaked from Pec-Pec's mouth, and Linny obeyed. The dragon fish disappeared into his mouth and Pec-Pec swallowed. The magician swayed his head meditatively until his braids formed a curtain over his face. He placed the side of his head on the rim of the fishbowl, and the audience heard a tiny *plop*. The dragon fish had fallen from the magician's ear.

* * *

Lights out at Camp Blade had been hours before, but Pec-Pec's night was not done. One kerosene lamp illuminated his tiny home, the back of a battered city-style delivery truck. The juggling torches were fitted with new burn rags and packed away. He had downed two bowls of his fiery bean soup and rinsed the utensils. The two wallets appropriated during the night's performance were plucked empty and now were under a foot of mud in the parking lot. The folding chairs and stage were strapped to the truck's roof, and the water and fuel tanks were full. The magician was ready to vanish. Almost.

Tapestries covered the walls. His folding cot was open, comforter, blankets, and pillow in place. He sat on the edge wearing a black robe, the fishbowl on his knees.

"Dragon fish, will you come with me?"

The fish was a prize, undeniably. But the longer he rambled the countryside with the glowing water-being, the more he came to feel awed, even uneasy, about its surreal talents.

Pec-Pec dipped in with both hands and drew the creature to his lips. He sucked it in, savoring the coppery taste. The patterns in the tapestries danced, then dissipated, and the truck fell away. He was the moon now: He could go where the moon went, know what the moon knew.

Summer night in little mud rut Camp Blade. Bodiless, Pec-Pec wafted down the boardwalk. He imagined himself an invisible air-fish, gently stroking his way through the cool pine-scent breezes. A barracks: snores and disinfectant and masturbation. He came to an empty bunk room, the thin mattress rolled, shelves robbed clean. For an hour, Pec-Pec studied every bared bedspring, every rent and stain and odor of the mattress, the microscopic particles of a minuscule dust storm playing across the floorboards—the leavings, the evidence and imprint of a man gone. Anton Takk had disappeared.

5
Information

Anton Takk awoke in a pillowed, perfumed luxury like he had never known before. At his feet a superfluous brass bed rail arced over vertical supports in decorative decadence. An acre of quilt, it seemed, blanketed his body in little squares fitted together neatly by invisible stitches.

He arose naked and studied the giant porcelain basin and its two spigots. The walls of the building, he realized, were webbed with pipes carrying water, hot and cold, to every room. He turned the spigot handles.

On the door was a notice in small print, tacked in each corner:

1. No spitting.
2. This room may not be used for any purpose considered illegal or immoral by the Government.
3. Guests checking out after noon may be charged for an extra day.

One hundred centimes a day for a room and still they treat customers like that!

Is it assumed, he wondered, that anyone who could afford a hotel room could read? Had things gotten that permissive in the cities—blocks of text posted anywhere you please? Or was it that most of the hotel's customers were Government? His mood darkened, and he tried to fight off paranoia. He regarded the sign again and satisfied himself with a tentative answer: You loosen one rule so that you can publicize three new ones.

Takk slid into the thrumbling warm water. The side of the tub was cool against his back and a scant film of sand scraped at his buttocks. He imagined himself to be a large pestle grinding away in the mortar of some giant's pharmacy. Takk resisted the return of drowsiness, feeling guilty about the splendor and the waste of time when he should be out gathering information.

There was a single thump at the door, and Takk's sleepiness vanished. He turned to face the door, sloshing the rising water. It could have been a clumsy passerby bumping a swinging duffel. Or? Who would know, especially this fast, where to find him? Ben Tiggle might hazard a good guess, but he would never tell the Badgers.

There came another rap, harder.

"Who?" said Takk.

The knob turned, and Takk began to understand the importance of hotel door locks. Ach, big cities! A slender man entered wearing a blue velvety tunic belted at the waist. He was clean-shaven, from the top of his head to his chin, except for an odd ponytail of wispy hair protruding from his left temple. It was a costume that Takk took to be fashionable on the streets of New Chicago, and it made him laugh—in less vulnerable situations.

"I am a friend," the stranger said.

"No, not a friend."

"Friendly, then," the intruder said, closing the door and seating himself on the edge of the bed. "You want some information."

Takk sucked in a breath. What was this, telepathy? He turned off the tub faucets and considered getting out of the water but did not.

"I'm just a tired tourist from the Northlands," Takk said

slowly, "trying to take a bath. A city map costs half a centime. That I have, and that's all the information I need. If I need a guide—"

"Enough," interrupted the bald man. "Say what you like—I don't give a poke for what your real story is. But you care about mine, I'll boogie. That is, if you want to stay out of jail."

Takk felt panic rising. He studied the little man's bulky tunic, wondering if it hid any weapons. New Chicagoans seemed to be smaller than Northlanders, somewhat sickly— perhaps something to do with in-breeding, Takk told himself. Warmer weather didn't really shrink people, did it?

"Go on," Takk said, sitting forward in the tub.

"Well, I'm at risk with the authorities, y'unnerstand," the stranger said. "They'll be not happy not to find you. I need a thousand centimes, I think, for the information."

"A thousand!"

The intruder's friendliness fell away as he bolted from the bed. "Prison, muscle boy!" he said, face reddening. He pointed a quivering index finger. Takk gagged at the sweetness of his cologne. "And I'll tell ya this much for free: I own three garages in town—private garages, discreet garages. When I study my logs for new customers, what do I find but—hooo, boogie—a Government registration number! Now what's a Government truck doing in a private garage? Unless it's stolen? And it's all full of dry food and outdoor gear and fuel tanks and old marked-up maps and— hah—books!"

"You entered the truck?"

"Oh, I just hear such a tale, that's all." He bared his teeth in a hard, exaggerated grin, his lips pushed back into a yellowish rectangle.

Matter-of-factly, Takk rose from the tub and strode toward the desk against the far wall, leaving footprint-shaped puddles.

"And that's all there really is to the story, right?" said Takk. "A thousand centimes for your silence?"

"A thousand."

Takk pulled back the heavy oak chair as if to open the top desk drawer. He gauged the chair's weight, then grasped

it by its right arm. With a sharp grunt, Takk hurled the chair
over the bed toward that bald dome with the surprised eyebrows.

A decade ago a hard-charging executive named Gould
Papier was assigned a building project expected to be, literally, the height of his career: construction of the largest
building in New Chicago, a five-story tower that would
house all of the city's Government offices. The new structure
would be a monument to Governmental principles: power,
efficiency, solidity.

Papier decided that the traditional building materials,
quarried stone or yellow brick salvaged from "old" Chicago, would not do; he needed a progressive and spectacular
medium, and he eliminated from his board of architects
those who seemed mired in the past. After months of bick-
ering, the panel arrived at poured, reinforced concrete, a
technique well known to the high-ticket builders: There were
said to be two miles of poured concrete sidewalks in the
affluent neighborhoods of New Chicago. It was not an unknown material in some buildings' foundations. Never before, however, had it been used on such a grand scale.

For eighteen months a model of the new Government
office building occupied a corner of his desk. It resembled
a pyramid, with eight concrete buttresses sweeping skyward, one at each corner and one on each side. Papier
pictured the building as a mighty, ribbed volcano. The
model gathered dust, anchored contract papers and requi-
sition forms, and, after its newness wore off, held pencils
in its center well.

No Government workers were surprised, privately, when
the final structural work on the Governmental center pushed
past its deadline in November that year: What ever really
got done *on time?* The last of the concrete was poured in
the ripping, icy winds of late December.

The first appreciable thaw came on March 21. Grateful
construction workers plastering walls and installing plumbing fixtures stripped down to their tattoos in the sudden
warmth of the bright morning. T-shirts, sweaters, and coats
littered all five tiers. Raucous guffaws and oft-repeated

punchlines to forgotten jokes rang freely up and down the corridors.

The concrete supporting the top two floors of the building, poured in the December freeze, actually never had achieved its intended rocklike state. It was poured into a mold as a liquid, of course, and rather than drying and hardening as the builders expected, the fluid concrete just froze. When Gould Papier's volcano melted, twenty-three workers died.

Gould Papier, "promoted" often these days within the shifting sediment of bureaucracy, occupied an office with a door labeled TRANSPORT: PUBLIC INFORMATION. His pocked face was drained of color; his hair, combed back, was yellow-gray. When a tall, rough-clothed figure lumbered through the door, Papier had been waiting patiently.

"Look, friend," the man approaching Papier's desk said. "Don't *you* tell me this is the wrong place. I've been out at the front desk, to this office, that office—and across town twice. Why the Government doesn't put all of its offices in the same—"

"Please," said Papier, closing his eyes, the bureaucrat's demand for silence.

Anton Takk looked around the barren room and sat in an oak chair of familiar design. Papier opened his eyes and studied the man before him. The jackboots alone gave him away as a Northlander, not to mention the thick black beard (with occasional starbursts of silver) or the ill-fitting denim work pants.

"Information," Papier said. "You want information."

Takk felt sweat burn its way to his brow.

"This is the *office* of information, for Transport anyway, and what I can't tell you perhaps my logbooks will." He motioned toward the wall of books over his shoulder. "And then there's always the telephone. So relax. Perhaps this is your last office for the day. What would you like to know?"

"I am looking for a friend."

"In Transport? Or Supply division? An employee?"

"A prisoner. In Transport, I guess. Right?"

"His name?"

"Her. Nora Londi. Came through here maybe year ago. Several months, sure."

Papier stood and faced the bank of logbooks. He perused the row of bindings and pulled one out from a floor-level shelf. "Are you a relative, by the way? Technically, this information should go only to relatives."

"Name's John," Takk said, and Papier's eyebrows rose. "Uh, John Justin. I'm just passing through. Fellow I work with up north says to be engaged to Nora Londi, is all. We're up logging, don't get around much. Said he'd be appreciative if I could find out anything."

"You would have travel papers, I suppose."

"Travel papers? *Oh!*" Takk unzipped his fly and drew out a flat wallet. He flipped his thumb across a layer of crinkly purple centime notes and pulled out a folded white square. Papier glanced at the form and handed it back.

The information officer silently skimmed the columns of his large logbook, at times turning back and forth through hundreds of pages, following numerous cross-references. Finally, he slammed the book shut, and his visitor felt the vibration in the floorboards. Papier returned the book to the gap in the shelf and took his seat again.

"In fairness," Papier said, "your friend should be warned, gently, that these women, umm, make extensive use of their physical attributes—for money, security, favors, whatever. Some have fiancées in each sector!"

"Where is Nora Londi?"

"Out to Sector 4, a prison mining camp called Blue Hole."

As Takk left, Papier noticed a large lock of human hair tied to a side belt loop of the Northlander's jeans. It looked like a ponytail.

Papier turned to the telephone. Ah, the exquisite Government tool—quick, efficient, and, if need be, anonymous and faceless. Definitely not to be trusted to the general population.

He wondered whether to give Takk a head start. Perhaps he was already being tailed by Security, and in that case Papier's supervisor would be expecting a prompt briefing.

Papier counted another twenty seconds, lifted the receiver, and dialed four numbers. "Sir . . . I gave him the information. . . . Yes. . . . It was Anton Takk. And there's something I didn't expect: He has travel papers. . . . No, an impeccable forgery."

The streets of New Chicago were covered with a malodorous layer of mud and horse dung. To Anton Takk's mind, however, it was hardly an inconvenience, especially on the main thoroughfares, which were bolstered by reliable paving stones, submerged though they were. (In Camp Blade, a man could lose his horse to a bog on Main Street in certain seasons.) New Chicago's pedestrians were an entertainment: The daintier among them would remove their glistening shoes, wade barefoot across the intersections, then rinse their feet in troughs at the other side. Enterprising urchins, grubby and brown-toothed, were at each corner charging an entire centime for a few moments' use of aged jackboots similar to Takk's, only much more tattered and probably leaking.

Many of the downtown buildings, some of them two or three stories tall, butted directly against one another, and it was often impossible to tell where one ended and the next began. The procession of horse carts, mule wagons, roaring trucks, and the occasional honking passenger car created a mind-numbing cacophony.

Takk hurried past the hotel. He had paid for two more nights, locked the door to room 24, and hung the SLEEPING sign on the doorknob. But he ducked his head to avoid recognition nevertheless, on the off chance that someone had entered his room and found a little man gagged and hanging by his wrists and ankles from the arcing bed rail.

Away from downtown, the streets were no longer at right angles to one another, and Takk navigated by a series of landmarks he had memorized: El Mercado, a sad little grouping of vendors' booths; the Juke, apparently a bar, with a black doorway he had no thought of entering; Happy's Hardware, where Takk lingered over the nails and chains and wire spools, and made a few purchases from the sour-faced store owner; and finally the garage, a wood-frame hulk of a building with a tiny office at the street front and ten sets of double doors stretched along the side alley.

Takk stopped at the fourth set of doors and released the ground bolts and latches. He wished he had used a padlock, but wasn't sure it would have done any good. The disarray in the Supply truck confirmed that it had been searched. Not much was missing—one of the lamps—it was hard to say what else. If the garage owner had expected a bribe he would have had to return the cargo fairly intact.

Takk flipped open a toolbox and selected a screwdriver, then walked around to the cab. The long seat cushion was mounted on a metal frame held in place by ten screws, which Takk removed. He heaved the seat up and forward. In the compartment below Takk found a flat bundle of burlap undisturbed, and he exhaled a relieved sigh. He laid the package on the cab seat and opened it. His hands were shaking. Takk eyed the garage doors. He returned to the back of the truck, took the remaining lamp, and lit it, then pushed the garage doors shut.

Inside the burlap were bundles of centime notes, which he brushed aside, revealing a cardboard notebook. He took the notebook in both hands and turned it over, letting the papers inside fall forward. They were crisp documents, freshly printed and very authentic looking. He didn't want to touch them with greasy hands. From the back of the notebook he drew another newly minted item, a white metal rectangle with raised lettering: A7279-88CB. Takk spat on the plate and rubbed the saliva over its entire surface, the grime from his hands darkening the fresh paint. He spat again, then scraped dirt from the garage floor and sprinkled that over the plate as well.

At the back of the truck, the first three bolts in the license plate came away grudgingly and the last one, in the bottom right corner, was rusted fast. Takk dripped oil on the stubborn bolt and struggled with screwdriver and monkey wrench until the bolt head was hopelessly torn. Droplets of sweat formed on the tip of his beard. He glanced at the door.

Takk bent the old license plate, forming a crease in the metal near the unmovable bolt. He bent the plate again and again along the same crease. Eventually it would break, and he would have to live with a corner of the old plate permanently affixed to the back of the truck. Maybe the new plate would cover it.

When he drove out of the garage a new lock and chain from Happy's Hardware clattered from the back door handles. At the end of the alley, Takk saw that a small crowd had gathered across the street beside a delivery truck. There was a small wooden stage, and a dark-skinned man with braided hair was juggling flaming torches.

6
Interrogation

Ben Tiggle was dreaming. Or was he? There was just blackness. His eyes itched, but he couldn't scratch. His limbs were numb and immobile. How many days had it been? That smell was in the room again, a sickly sweet floral cologne, which meant that the voice would come too, and there it was, that polite Southlander twang:

"Mr. Tiggle. . . . Ben Tiggle."

"Unnnh. Morning."

"Oh, morning, is it? Well, perhaps it is. Perhaps not. You were telling me about the money, Mr. Tiggle. How much money does Anton Takk have?"

"I dunno. Dunno."

"You *gave* him money."

"A hunnerd . . . hunnerd 'n' fifty centimes."

"That's hardly enough for a long-distance trip, Mr. Tiggle."

"He said it was a loan. Skipped out on me, the pig shit."

"A small loan, Mr. Tiggle. Not enough to get upset about. Are you sure it wasn't more?"

"Maybe someone else . . ."

"Did you teach Anton Takk to read?"

"I can't read!"

"Oh, come now. We can all read, *some,* can't we? Isn't it just a matter of degree? *I* can read. . . ."

"You're Government."

"We're all Government." The voice paused. "Now, I suppose you can read numbers, right? To do your books. You run a warehouse, so you must read crate labels . . ."

"I just open the bastards."

". . . and fill out requisitions. . . ."

"Nah. I just take what they send me."

"Did you help Mr. Takk steal the truck? It was a Supply truck, last known to be at your loading dock."

"Anton's loading dock."

"He just helped himself to your warehouse and you knew nothing about it?"

"Yeah. Told ya, he works there. *Worked* there."

"Where did he go?"

"Dunno. Probably he just went for a ride. He'll be back sooner or later. He's crazy like that. But this is the craziest."

"Do you think Anton Takk is crazy? Um, unbalanced?"

"Yeah . . . well, no. He's usually real quiet, a good kid. Real quiet, good kid. Then one day he'll do something stupid."

"Is Anton Takk stupid?"

He exhaled heavily. "Nah. Naïve."

"The day he disappeared, a Badger named Krieger was found dead—beaten to death in his bed."

"A sour bastard. Lots of enemies. Lots."

"We think Takk might have done it and then panicked. Perhaps he hadn't had the nerve to run until he'd murdered a Badger."

No answer.

"Do you think Anton Takk might need special treatment?"

"Like I'm getting?"

"Do you think Mr. Takk might need hospital care—for emotional disorders?"

No answer.

"Did you raise Anton Takk?"

"Some. His father, John Justin Takk, disappeared . . ."

"Died."

". . . died. Long time ago." Tiggle shook his head. He had lost his equilibrium and felt as if he were reeling through darkness. He wanted to rub his eyes. They itched. He thought of sappy pine needles pressed to his face.

"So you would play with him at free time?"

"Yeah."

"Dress him for bed?"

"Yeah."

"Maybe tuck him in and read him a story?"

"Yeah."

"Where is the press, Mr. Tiggle?"

"The press?"

"Printing press. Anton Takk had access to a printing press. Where is it?"

"In Camp Blade? Ridiculous. Look around. Where would we hide it?"

"We?"

"Anyone."

There was silence. After a few minutes Ben Tiggle's head lolled to one side and his breathing became slow and steady.

"Mr. Tiggle."

"Oh. Hmn. Good morning."

"Morning, is it? Perhaps. Mr. Tiggle, would you like to see again?"

"Please. My eyes itch. Let me up."

"Mr. Tiggle, do you know what happens when someone has his eyelids sewn shut? When tiny incisions are made across them . . ."

"What?"

"The human body's healing process is amazing, Mr. Tiggle. The eyelids grow together. A graft. It takes a week or ten days."

"How long have I been here?"

"You were telling me about the money. . . ."

7
Loo

Loo was stretched along a branch of a spruce tree like a large cat dozing. From the tree, she could meditate on the world. The river whispered below—so far down that its red-brown banks appeared misted slightly, even on such a clear day with a shocking blue sky. To the east, the forested gorge walls marched stern and erect; to the west, the walls relaxed and widened, and the river spread into a finger lake, pushed up by a dam miles downstream. The sunlight, mottled by the branches above, warmed Loo's bare skin, countering the cool breeze pressing steadily at her face.

Out of habit, Loo's gaze followed a gust of wind traveling up the canyon wall in a dark, fluttering swath across the sparse treetops. She imagined diving into the burst of wind at just . . . the right . . . moment . . . *there*. The gust rattled the branches of her spruce and quickly subsided.

Her attention returned dutifully to the waterfall emptying into the foot of the finger lake directly below. To the untrained eye it was a pristine monument to nature, untouched by mankind. But the boulders bordering the river at the top of the waterfall were the first clue to the work of a calculated hand: They formed, a little too neatly, a funnel that channeled the river into a concentrated, powerful stream of water and foam gushing over the waterfall's crest. More discreet, however, nearly invisible through the spray, was a cylindrical paddlewheel spinning under the cascade, a turbine whose shaft disappeared into the gorge walls on either side.

A dark flickering caught Loo's eye, and she squinted. There was something in the protective net spanning the length of the turbine, not a log or branch. Something, some *things* squirming in the manmade spiderweb. Maybe something for dinner?

Loo drew herself up to her knees, dragged her harness out of the branches below, and strapped it to her shoulders and waist. She slipped her arms through the loops under the pair of skin-covered wing frames and twisted the grab-handles to check the steering action. Satisfied, she bounced once on the branch, dived headlong into the gorge, and spread her wings.

In more casual circumstances, when pride could be a factor, Loo would spend two hours circling her way to the gorge bottom, finally coming to rest only as the result of fatigue or boredom, not for lack of skill at catching new updrafts. But this was urgent, possibly, and she cocked her wings back and tilted into a steep downward spiral, covering the same distance in minutes.

As she fell, Loo opened her lungs and released a repeating birdlike howl: "Oo-ooong, oo-ooong, oo-ooong. . . . " The echoes caromed back from the north and south gorge walls and overlapped each other. To those who knew the language, it was a warning, probably more of an alarm than the situation merited. But to Loo the resounding call added another layer of exhilaration to the rapid descent, quite worth the admonishment that she risked from the elders later on.

Loo ended her flight with a dive toward the center of the waterfall, an attack she cut short with a sharp dip up to kill her air speed. She settled lightly on the outermost rope of the net guarding the turbine—a precise move she hoped had been noticed from the banks of the lake. When she unbuckled two shoulder straps and removed her arms from their

loops, the wings fell flat against her back, giving her the
look of a large, slender insect. Loo crouched and grabbed
the netting for balance. The ropes, slippery and green with
algae, were woven hemp the thickness of her wrists.

A dozen yards down the slope of netting the white column
of water pounded through the rigging and sent up through
the ropes a perpetual vibration. Loo quickly surveyed the
captives: several pack llamas wriggled helplessly but safe,
their cries inaudible amid the water thunder; a figure under
the cascade lay inert, possibly already drowned; and a mon-
strous human, a woman easily twice Loo's size, was awkwardly crawling toward the net's rim. She wore clothes—
impossibly confining garments, Loo observed—in the way
of all outsiders.

So the woman giant was the only immediate problem:
For one thing, she carried a rifle in one hand as she scrambled and slipped and clawed up the net. Second, and most
important, once she reached the edge of the net would she
have the poise not to fall into the turbine and damage it?
Loo, not willing to take this risk, pulled a leather sling from
a narrow slot in her right wing frame. From inside her right
cheek she drew a green, moist object, which she placed in
the sling's pocket.

Loo's lilting bird cry "Oo-oong" caught the giant's attention. The crawling woman's head jerked up and she
pulled her matted red hair out of sight's way. Oddly, the
face brightened, seemingly out of relief or recognition rather
than surprise. Loo had thought her prey might bolt for the
net's edge and dive. There was a whish-snap of leather as
Loo flailed the sling, and the outsider scratched at her neck,
where a tiny, slippery thing clung to the area of her jugular.
The large woman pulled the object away and had barely
enough time to focus on it—a minuscule snake with over-
sized fangs—before she collapsed into the slimy netting.

Loo returned the sling to its slot and stepped nimbly down
the net, quite adjusted to the quivering of the slick ropes.
She took the rifle first, having to pull the large woman's
clammy fingers from the stock. Loo found the little snake

in the woman's other hand, stroked the tiny animal until it seemed numbed, then returned it to the wet warmth of her cheek. With her free hand, Loo set about a complex series of maneuvers to turn her limp captive around. She yanked first at one soggy pant leg and then the other until, finally, the giant's legs were elevated higher than her head. In that position, with one simple slice at the neck, the body would drain itself neatly into the lake. It would be many pounds lighter when it came time to lower it to the beach.

From a slot in her left wing frame Loo drew a slender blade. It was a flier's knife, thin, lightweight, and easy for a careless user to break—nothing near the heft of the cutters to be found in the town below. Loo took pride in the longevity of her knives, and this one had lasted her months despite all of its use. The giant body lay facedown, and Loo planted a bare foot on the woman's shoulder, forcing the chest back and exposing the neck. She studied the hammy arms and large breasts rolling under the wet shirt. No waste in this, she thought. Never could this one fly.

There was a leather collar in the way, with a smaller strip of leather wound over it several times. Inured to the peculiar costuming of the outsiders, Loo worked her knife under the collar with no thought to saving it. She pulled up, and the strapping separated and fell away.

As Loo crouched to make the final, neat slash across the throat, she spotted something on the woman's chest that stung like an electric charge. It was a red metal rectangle, undoubtedly a sign of the Government, pinned crookedly to her shirt. Suddenly near tears, Loo stood and glanced up and down the banks in fear that someone might have witnessed her mistake. The slim knife fell from her hands, bounced on a green rope, and fell into the whirling turbine.

8
The Doll Collection

Pec-Pec sat cross-legged on the cot in the back of his truck, surrounded by the intricate tapestries. His head was nodded, the braids forming curtains on either side of his face.

Outside were the rolling plains that stretched south of New Chicago. On the other side of a nearby rise ran a ribbon of ruined interstate highway. It was barely passable during the day; now, with the sun falling, there would be no more passersby, no sane ones anyway.

A slate of low, swirling clouds was sliding across the early summer sky unnaturally fast. Occasionally a twisting gray cone would lower itself from the flat cloud layer, a crosswind threatening to grow into a tornado. Pec-Pec had seen the baby cyclones and decided to ignore them, pulling the truck doors closed.

Balanced before him on the stretch of cot canvas was a large bullet, standing on end five inches high. He had purchased the ghastly banger just this afternoon. Driving out of New Chicago, in pursuit of Anton Takk, he had passed a row of salvagers' booths—box after box, bin after bin, table after table laden with metal and plastic scraps of a civilization long since erased from the continent.

He had fallen instantly ill as he passed the booths, as if there were a putrid gas in his stomach, and he stopped. Instinctively, he pawed through the mounds of tarnished and dirt-caked objects, feeling sicker the closer he came. In that way, he homed in on it quickly, at once repulsed and yet determined to find the foul source—a single, ugly rifle bullet among the bent gears and nameless twisted shards in the bottom of a cardboard carton.

"Ah doubt she'd a bang off, even if you'd a found a proper firing instrument for her," said the salvager behind that table, a ragged woman with a cancer eating at her nose.

Bullets not far different from this one, newly manufactured ones, had done much harm to his people—land wars, mostly, and enslavement for the Southland farms. But this vile piece had seemed to have an evil unto itself, burning cold as he rolled it between his fingers. What it meant, he did not know yet, but he had to have the bullet. Pec-Pec paid the hag twenty centimes.

So now he meditated over the bullet in the back of his truck. He had surrounded it with four tiny clay figures, carefully sculpted and painted, human-shaped dolls scarcely an inch in height. The burly, red-haired doll with the bulb nose was the wanderer named Nora Londi. She was the key, the spearhead. The slender, rangier doll with the graying beard was the antsy Northlander Anton Takk. He would have to follow Londi, and in so doing would draw out the other two—the grayhead with the mangled hand, Rosenthal Webb, and the young one, the blond assistant Gregory. He had chosen each carefully for their parts like a chef devising a new recipe. It was not so much a scientific method of selection. It was more like satisfying an inner hunger that he could never put into words.

Pec-Pec stared at the circle of dolls around the bullet, hoping for a meaning. His eyes did not move from one to another, but he took in all of the figures at once, as a whole.

The minutes lapsed into hours, and still the magic man did not move. As he stared, a series of shooting stars streaked across his vision until he saw nothing but a mesh of fine tracer lights. The lines then melded together into a pulsing ball of glowing red, rhythmic—bright, then dark, bright again, dark.

When Pec-Pec's vision finally cleared that night, the pulse remained in the form of sound, a throb so low that it was almost beyond human perception. It faded until he could not distinguish it from his heartbeat.

And Pec-Pec had his answer—not a big one, a small answer. Rhythm, sound. Music.

The magic man fell to his knees on the truck floor and pulled a jar from under the cot. He spun off the top, pulled out a tiny wad of clay, and rolled it in his hands. He pinched into the clay a head, two arms, two legs. With a small wooden stylus he began shaping a face he did not yet know.

Music. Hmmm. Where would he find a musician willing to lay siege to the Government?

9
Moberly Inn

It was a thundering and wet morning when Anton Takk pulled off the road—two lanes of asphalt chunks, gravel, and mud—and followed red-on-white hand-painted signs to the Moberly Inn. Takk's eyes burned. The rolling hills were becoming more pronounced in this territory, and a lapse in concentration could be fatal. The driver's-side window was lowered two inches (the temperature had risen ten degrees since he had left New Chicago), and the cool air and spray of rain on his face were all that kept him from sleep. He rolled down a drive even more poorly maintained than the highway he had just left. Thorny branches slapped at the front of the truck, leaving teardrop-shaped leaves to be brushed aside by the windshield wipers.

When Takk chugged into a hilltop clearing he found what appeared to have once been a farmhouse. The ancient central structure was a staid two-story wood frame building with several haphazard additions spoking off from it. A barn on the far side of the house seemed to serve as the motor shed. On the barn roof, a haphazard antenna wavered in the wet wind. There was a fuel pump and a squat water tank with thick steel legs sunk into concrete. A truck with Government license plates was parked beside the barn, flanked by two jeeps, a van, and a pickup truck. Takk was not as far from the mainstream of traffic as he had hoped.

"*I'm* Moberly," said the woman behind the counter inside. "Ain't no 'mister' here t'all . . . *Mister*."

"I really am sorry," Takk said, leaning his duffel against the front of the counter. "I need a room for a while."

There were four tables spread about a large threadbare Oriental rug in the front room, which had once been a living room. Three of the tables were occupied with people consuming breakfast—grits, ham, eggs, coffee, biscuits. Takk heard a snicker behind him, but he did not turn to look.

"You're driving Supply, are you?" asked Moberly. She had streaks of gray in her black hair, not unlike Takk, and wings of fine wrinkles flaring out from each eye.

"Yes."

"Fifteen centimes a day. Room five's down yonder." She pointed toward a dark hallway leading into one of the newer additions. She handed him a key, and Takk decided to use it this time.

Takk unzipped his pants and withdrew the wallet. He counted out three five-notes and lay them on the counter. Moberly's eyes rolled toward the ceiling. She quickly folded the notes in half and discreetly tucked them into a pants pocket. She cocked her head toward the door behind her.

"If yer needin' a spare fuel pump, we'll have ta junk around for a minute in the workroom," she said, disappearing through the door. "Come around," she shouted.

Fuel pump? The truck was running fine. Or had someone been tampering with it already? Was this another shakedown of some kind? He grabbed his duffel and followed the woman into the work room. Moberly closed the door behind him.

"How you got this far, Mister, I dunno," Moberly said. "But you're a runner and a liar and a thief."

Takk rubbed his eyes, wondering if he would have to dash for the truck. He had not refueled yet—a stupid mistake—and he tried to remember what the gas gauge had read. "What are you talking about? I just need a room. My money's good. . . ."

"Well, that's the number-one right there," Moberly huffed, keeping her voice low. "Your money. A Government man pays by Government chit. Cash? Hah!"

"Hey, I'm new—just hired. Don't even have all my papers yet."

Moberly's face softened, and she walked farther into the room. The workroom was a maze of ceiling-high shelves burdened with items in disrepair—coils of ragged wire, engine parts, plumbing fixtures, gears, unidentifiable machinery, and the odor of rust and oil. Takk followed. Moberly stopped at one shelf and poked at the keys of an antique adding machine that was missing its metal shell.

"Most of the Supply drivers—the real ones—trade on the side," she said. "Maybe tobacco or coffee, maybe machinery. The nervy ones—maybe even books, although I'd never touch 'em." She glanced up at Takk and turned away again. "One day some guy's gonna come in with an adding machine just like this—only it'll have a full set of key springs, which this one doesn't. Or somebody'll have drive belts 'n' gaskets for that generator in the corner. That'd be nice—another generator."

"Yeah," said Takk. "Another generator. That'd be nice." Takk began to wonder about her emotional stability.

"So the more bits and pieces you have," Moberly said, "the better chance you have of puttin' things together. The more parts you have that'll fit someday. You, you're a liar and a runner. And whatever you're running from or after, that's the one thing you have and, well, of course you don't *have* it. Or you wouldn't be running."

"I'd just like a room, please. That's what I'd like to have."

"You have a room," she said. "Just be gone before daylight tomorrow. And stay away from the guests. Some of 'em are Government—real Government—and *all* of 'em like to gossip."

Takk shrugged, trying to look as if he did not understand, and turned for the door.

"You don't have long, you know," she said to his back.

Takk stopped and watched her pick her way to a metal box the size of an oil drum. The upper face of the casing bore four rows of faded keys and a plexiglass panel that protected the emerging paper. Moberly tapped her finger on the smudgy print.

"Anybody with a wireless knows your description, that you killed a Badger. And nobody hides in this world—nobody."

10
A New Mission

"Rosenthal Webb, you are fifty-five years old. You tend to limp when the humidity's high—we've all seen it." Virginia Quale motioned around the conference table. "We agreed to this mission—with much debate and mountainous reservations—and, well, I'm sorry, but there are younger and stronger men. They have more endurance and agility. It's hard fact, Rose." She flushed. "Rosenthal. And you're a man of hard facts."

Webb, too, was reddening. A tiny wildfire was spreading across his cheeks and forehead and he was helpless to stop it. He detested what he thought of as Quale's motherly nature. And with logic on her side it was all the more exasperating. His words came slowly, in measured tones calculated to sound frighteningly controlled, as if any more resistance might bring an explosion of fury. His being eliminated from one mission was not the only thing at stake—if he lost this one, he would never be granted another. Cranking windmills for the rest of his life.

"I am aging," he said. "Yes, by plumb, I am. You could not really say that I am going soft, though. I am strong. I work out daily, even through the winter. You all know that. The younger men, well, most of what they know about fieldwork they have learned from me and they have a small fraction of my experience.

"And there is the matter of our field contacts, people who have known me for years. Some of them only I am aware of; they will deal with no one else." He pointed for emphasis with his left index finger, and seven sets of eyes followed the motion. "We are privileged with an insulated existence. We can forget that out *there*, in real life, trusting a stranger is risking your life."

"May I interject?" asked Winston Weet. "I grant you the physical ability, even if some at our table will not. I am older than you, Rosenthal, and I *am* soft. And I concede the need for the mission, and I voted for it. I don't doubt that Takk is bumbling badly and is about to be caught, *or* that he will very likely take some good people down with him. But I want to bring up another point. I am a scientist, and perhaps I consider causes and effects differently from some people and—oh, that doesn't really matter." Weet cleared his throat. "What do you say to the skeptic who wonders if you didn't create the need for this mission in the first place? You *did* send Anton Takk a wheelbarrow load of money."

Webb stood and pushed his chair back. Virginia Quale flinched, and Webb himself wondered if he could refrain from shouting. "The money," Webb said, "merely served as assistance to a project already set in motion by Anton Takk. The young man is very resourceful. He had an entire warehouse at his disposal. He even has the services of a printing press for forgeries.

"But money, I gully, from what Takk said in the letter, was going to be a problem. From our distance, it was the assistance that could travel fastest without being detected— a coded wireless transmission to New Chicago, and from there, the actual money was hidden in a direct shipment to Camp Blade. Money—it was juss five thousand centimes, not 'a wheelbarrow load'—is the most versatile of tools for what Takk was needing to do. But anyway, no—it's a situation of Takk's creation."

"You seem to take Takk's letter at face value now," said Quale.

"I have believed all along that the essence of the letter is true," answered Webb, "although I am aware of a couple of blatant lies—probably used to protect friends."

"What lies?"

"Well, about Ben Tiggle for one—the warehouse manager." Webb's face darkened. "I have known him for a long . . . long . . . time. Now he has disappeared."

"I do wish Mr. Takk had just stayed put," Quale said.

"Virginia," Webb responded, "you're starting to sound like the Government."

II
A New Assignment

Lunch at Subbo's Restaurant, considered that month to be New Chicago's most stylish dining spot, was being paid for by the Government. That fact was the only thing about the meeting that Gould Papier did not find distasteful. To Papier's left sat his boss, an obese senior deputy of Transportation named Glenn Wig, who was known to be quite indiscreet in public with his flatulence—both physical and verbal. Wig was ordering another bottle of the house red wine.

The other man at the table was a stranger, a Security officer introduced to him as Inspector Mick Kerbaugh, a slender man who seemed to Papier to represent the opposite of Wig's characteristics but in an equally detestable way. Kerbaugh bore a stylish left-temple ponytail (did no one dare wear one on the right side?), and the rest of his head, apparently shaven just that morning, formed a large angular dome. There were two pronounced flat surfaces, looking like armor plating, that made up the left and right sides of his forehead. Kerbaugh wore that popular, overbearing cologne that Papier likened to a physical assault, and his white cotton tunic ended fashionably at the knee.

Papier himself felt more at home with his yellow-gray hair combed back, and all of his tunics brushed the ankles modestly and ran to the darker colors. This was a way of dressing considered among New Chicago's older professionals to be satisfyingly unchic.

The Transport information officer had developed over the years a functional way of listening to his rotund boss's blatherings: Papier tended to daydream until certain important phrases were used, or until Glenn Wig employed a particular tone of voice that mustered his attention. And just then Papier found his sensibilities being roused from a daydream.

Wig was saying: "... and so then I says just this morning to the minister of Security, 'Hey, as a matter of fact I just got off the phone with my information officer an' he's had direct contact with this Anton Takk, seen him and smelled him in person—hah, I mean, he's a Northlander, right?— and what's more, my beloved Gould Papier knows the western sectors like he knows his own pud.' So Gould, did I serve you well on this one or what?"

"Well, I'm not sure, Mr. Wig. Just how did this conversation resolve itself?"

Wig leaned into the table toward Papier as if to deliver the punchline of a particularly bawdy joke. His second and third and fourth chins folded into one another like a compressed accordion. He downed the last of his wine and set the glass to the side just as the waiter was opening the new bottle.

"Are we being a little slow today, Papier?" asked the Transport deputy. He paused for a tiny belch, the fumes from which wafted toward his employee's nostrils. "We need a Transport official—someone of appreciable distinction and authority—to accompany Mr. Kerbaugh in his pursuit of this ne'er-do-well, Anton Takk. Not only is he a runner, but now comes to light that he's a murderer too."

Papier began to fidget, and Wig continued, "I believe you will find it a welcome relief from the rigors of your office duties. Think, Mr. Papier, what an opportunity to strike a highly visible blow for good and order—laying waste this reprobate!''

''Actually . . .'' Kerbaugh interrupted and let the silence hold court for a moment. From the single word, Papier recognized the hard-core Southlander twang, much thicker than would be found among most New Chicagoans. ''Our orders are not to lay waste anyone for the moment,'' the Security man continued. ''Primarily, we want to follow him closely and analyze how and why he makes every move. If an individual gives him aid, that individual must be incapacitated to prevent recurrences. If Government regulations are too lax, they must be improved. We have already found out, for instance, that Transport documents are being forged much too easily. Once we know who all of Mr. Takk's friends are, well . . .''

Wig fell back and his brow wrinkled defensively. ''You couldn't think that some Northland log-buster scratched out those Transport forms with a quill!''

''Of course not,'' said Kerbaugh. ''But the fact remains that a forger available to Takk has that capability, and we must change our systems and stay five steps ahead of the reprobates. I have already begun making inquiries into the location of the illicit press.''

''But what if I don't want this assignment?'' asked Papier.

''If that were so,'' responded Wig, ''I wouldn't be so unpatriotic as to say so. You and Mr. Kerbaugh are leaving town this evening. Please don't worry about your current duties, my boy. Tim Kittleworth is moving into your office right now—temporarily, of course.''

Glenn Wig then broke wind loudly, and all conversation in Subbo's Restaurant died. His two companions flipped open their menus simultaneously, and Papier wondered if he could manage to eat anything at all, whether or not it was paid for by the Government.

12
Inside a Pumpkin

Nora Londi awoke to the odor of wet fur, and she found that she had been using a llama for a pillow. The room was round and the walls curved outward, prompting Londi to imagine that she was inside a large pumpkin. Three round windows, too small to crawl through, let three beams of light into the room. The only other opening was a large circle in the center of the ceiling, and that, Londi decided, had to be the door. Except that there was no ladder.

Londi sat up groggily, head humming with pain, and scratched at the little scabs on her neck. She remembered something about a miniature snake. On the far side of the room a nude, dark-skinned woman crouched, her hands against the floor and her eyes attentive. Their gazes locked, and the crouching woman launched into an unintelligible monologue of sonorous syllables and a pleasing cadence: "Ooo-ooong, ooo-oonga . . ."

Londi listened for several minutes. There were three llamas in the room, behind her, and the one she had been sleeping against craned his neck up, mesmerized by the chanting woman's voice. This was the largest of the llamas, the one named Diego. He still wore the empty rifle holster.

The llama began to speak in a gutteral counter-rhythm, a hauntingly similar voice: "Hooorm, hooorma, hooorm, hooorma . . ." The woman against the wall responded, more enthusiastically than before, and the give-and-take quickly grew to a frantic, reverberating exchange.

"Hey," Nora Londi shouted, and the interplay stopped, leaving a ghostly echo. "Uh, sorry, but do you speak English? That's all I know."

The tiny woman seemed to understand the question. She shook her head from side to side and then opened her mouth to show what seemed in the half-light to be the stub of a mangled tongue. The dark woman flattened a palm against each cheek and rested, as if waiting for the next move. The llama Diego twisted his head in Londi's direction, regarding her for the first time.

"Damn," said Londi, massaging her forearms, "for a blue minute I thought you had a *conversation* going."

"A conversation," the llama responded. "A conversation going."

Londi rolled onto her shoulder away from Diego and came to rest in a squatting position much like Loo's. "What?" was all she could manage.

Diego's lips worked against each other meditatively. He settled closer to the floor and placed one forepaw over the other. "Human . . . talk," the llama said, his words clear yet halting and hollow sounding. "Many talks . . . I know. You make a sound, I make a sound just like."

Londi remained motionless, and her eyes darted between Diego and the small woman against the opposite wall, both of whom seemed unperturbed. Londi rocked back onto her rear and permitted herself a nervous laugh.

Diego repeated the laugh—same pitch, same cadence, a ghostly mirror of Londi's own voice. She had heard of this kind of thing, mimicry. But it only happened with birds, didn't it? And this seemed to be more than mindless repetition: The llama acted as if he had some idea of what he was saying—unless there was some remarkable training behind all of this, and the beast was just spewing words.

Loo bellowed three low-register hoots directed at the ceiling, and a rope ladder obediently fell from the hole above. She put the end of the ladder between her teeth, mounted the rungs, and as she climbed up she took the ladder with her.

There were murmurs from the other two llamas, nothing that Nora Londi understood.

"Where I come from the animals don't talk—in English, anyway," Londi said. "Maybe they're not that smart."

"Humans . . . talk."

"Oh, yeah."

"Humans," Diego said slowly, as if carefully selecting the words, "humans jabber, jabber, jabber. Other animals . . . less talk, more smart. You know, hooma . . . dogs?"

"I haven't owned one for years," Londi said, "but sure, I know what they are."

"Many dogs . . . talk two tongues, hoom. Own dogs, not good."

"What?"

"Own dogs, not good. Own llama, not good. Give llama a job, good. Own . . . not good."

"Good god," Londi muttered.

"Good god," Diego responded. "Good food. Good morning. Would you like Indians in your ambulance?"

"You're losing it, my friend." Londi was growing more sure that the llama had been trained by rote, perhaps as a joke. Then again, maybe this was all a creation of the snake venom in her blood.

Diego tried again. "A thing to say, hooma . . . in morning. Good morning. Would you like Indians . . . would you like onions in your . . . omelet?"

"Oh. Ah, no thanks, sport." Londi glanced around, but there was no food of any kind in the cell.

Diego lowered his head onto his paws and closed his eyes.

13
A Meeting

Anton Takk could smell the rain from where he lay. A long, flimsy curtain covered a row of three windows against the far wall, and the muted light told him that night was falling. The only sounds were the steady *dit-dit-dit* against the glass and, from somewhere in the building, a lazy mechanical *thunk, thunk, thunk* that would continue for ten minutes, stop, and start again. A noisy well pump, he supposed.

Takk had thrown the quilt aside and lay naked under the single cool sheet, drifting in and out of daydream. A light flashed across the window, and Takk suddenly was fully awake. An engine growled in the parking lot—not a truck, Takk told himself, but something smaller, a jeep, or perhaps a passenger car if any could make it this far.

He pulled the sheet away and crept to the edge of the curtain, avoiding the dying light. A canvas-topped jeep was pulling to a stop beside Takk's Supply truck. It was a Government jeep, but old and rusted enough to have been sold as surplus. Its headlights died, and two riders carrying bundles ran for the main house.

Someone would have to greet the first of the evening's

customers. Takk returned to the bed and walked across it on his knees to the sleeping figure on the other side. "Hey, Moberly," he said, and he pushed at the shoulder. "Some new arrivals. Hey, I'd like to know who they are."

There was a low groan and the figure rolled over. "I'm not Moberly," came a man's voice.

Takk sprang from the bed. He rapidly patted his hands over the dark surface of the dresser, knocking over an empty ale bottle, until he found the sheath of his hunting knife. He pulled a strap away from the handle and yanked out the blade.

"What are you doing here?"

"I am trying to sleep," said the stranger.

"Donna move. I have a knife."

"Yes," said the voice in the dark. "It's a beautiful instrument, carefully made—not a Government job at all. I was admiring it a while ago. You see, I am a friend."

"No, not a friend," said Takk, and he remembered the incident in his hotel room in New Chicago, where another man had claimed to be a friend.

Takk reached to the dresser again and found a striker match. He pulled the storm glass off of the dresser lamp and lit the wick. It was the torch juggler in his bed, the dark man with braided hair and thin mustache he had seen outside of the garage in New Chicago. Takk examined the door and, to his surprise, found its slide bolts still securely in place. Not only will I use room keys and bolts now, Takk told himself, but I'll be sleeping with my knife.

"My name is Pec-Pec," said the man, opening his large hands as if to prove them empty. The room began to smell of freshly ground coffee. "Did you know I've been following you? I get better at it all the time."

"Yeah, I seen—a few times, at least," he lied. "You're a gypsie or something, right?"

Pec-Pec looked disappointed. "I am a magic man. I travel and perform—I would quite literally die if I stayed in one place. I am to keep an eye on you, and it is the perfect duty for me. I go everywhere."

"Who says you must watch me, and why would a tourist

such as me need watching?" Takk was pulling on his trousers while still gripping the knife. He tucked his wallet into the pants and zipped the fly closed. The pants hung loosely on his hips. These gut frights, he thought, are sucking my life away.

"Oh, just good people"—Pec-Pec waved a hand—"out there, everywhere you go, really. The Government would call them conspirators, and they would call themselves, well, the un-Government. They gave you money, I understand, a substantial sum. You would know more about them, I think, except that the little place you come from—" Pec-Pec shrugged.

"Well, ho! How many know this tale?"

Pec-Pec's face furrowed with a frown. "Don't shout at me! You are the one that sent the letter—three copies did you say?"

"How many know?"

"Dozens, maybe. I found just one copy—bought it at a flea market in South-of-the-Bend after it was read aloud at auction. A warehouser's assistant had found it, was selling it as an amusement, a comedy. You can't blame him for thinking it a fiction. . . ."

"It's all true—well, mostly, the nut of it is. Parts, anyway. If I had a way of helping Nora Londi, I would do that. I know where she is now—Blue Hole. Huh. No one returns."

"But there is more, no?" Pec-Pec's voice was growing scornful. "Perhaps there is a restless younger here, a lifetime log-camp boy who would like to see those sprawling sectors that the travelers tell of? And perhaps this younger thinks he is going to pound a Badger to settle a hard score, and he needs money to bolt with? Hoo, well. No one's going to send money and maps for that, are they?"

Takk was reddening even more as he buttoned his shirt. "Why don't you get your own damned room? I might have killed ya—or died of a heart banger. And where's Moberly?"

"Moberly, dear Moberly, has been up for hours. She works alone, you know, and the travelers are starting to arrive. As for the other question—well, you don't expect me to pay for my own room, do you? Not when I could share a bunk with my new companion. A companion who has come into sudden wealth!''

"Oh, ya, 'new companion,' is it? No, this I am doing alone. I do not need some . . . some traveling circus to draw attention to me. And I *don't* have any money—nothing to kill for, anyway.''

Pec-Pec tossed the sheet aside and stood. He was fully dressed: denim trousers, boots, a blousy dark shirt run through with random red and gold threads. The magic man's face was grim. ''Anton Takk,'' he said, ''you could not have done a better job of drawing attention to yourself. I was not going to show myself to you at all, but now we have an emergency. You are about to be found, and there are more important things for you to do than die here.''

Takk pointed the knife at Pec-Pec's flared nose. ''I don' want to *do* anything. I want to be where no one knows me, is all. Maybe with your 'un-Governments'—where are they?''

''You will meet them, where we're going, when we do what needs doing.''

''What's this what needs doin'?''

Pec-Pec's eyes widened. ''Oh! Well, I don't know yet.''

Takk sniffed. ''I've known a few dark-fleshed men, up Camp Blade. Seen more in New Chicago. You ain't like any of 'em. You're not a natural bowl of beans, are ya?''

Pec-Pec tapped at his lips pensively with two fingers. ''How much of the truth can you stand?'' he asked.

''The truth that's, well, the *truth* —let's have all of that.''

''Ah, all of the truth,'' Pec-Pec said, settling back onto the bed. He leaned into a pillow and put his feet up. ''Let's see. Born in the Southlands, not far from the Big Ocean. Keep a home sometimes in the Out Islands, although I travel about mostly. I lend assist to the Rafers when I can, as your Government is not the most understanding . . .''

''Ho, the Rafers! Savages?''

''Umm. They wouldn't think much of you either, I 'spect.''

''But they file their teeth to a point, the better to eat babies, run 'round naked—''

Pec-Pec was waving his hand in the air. "I see this will take more time than we have here. But I must say to you a little about the Rafers. You know of the firebombs what landed in the Big War. Well, the radiation fields burn so strong for the first several decades that hunnerds—hoo—thousands of Southlanders were cut away from the population to which you were born. People known as blacks, Indians, Cajuns. Even a race called Texans. Now they are all Rafers.

"They don' gully your concept of ownership of territory. Huh. Their tribes prefer the distant lands, far from Government and its bangers—the plains, the Out Islands. . . ."

Takk was frowning. He scratched under his beard. Resigned, he nailed the knife into the dresser top, but stayed within reach. "Stop. Ho, you jabber on. I'm thinking of here and now, an' thass most of what I can care about. Here and now I . . . I . . . just . . . want . . . to disappear."

"Ya, okay." Pec-Pec was whispering now. "But not like your father disappeared. Not like that."

Moberly had sounded equally worried about Government pursuers.

"I don't suppose I can go back," Takk said. The ale, from hours before, smacked sour in his mouth now. "Not after I pounded a Badger. Hah. I wouldn't mind, I think, just staying here. Moberly—ach, I like her. But I don't suppose I can do that either."

"No," Pec-Pec said. "I don't suppose."

Takk doused the lamp and went to the window. Now there was yet another Supply truck, smaller than his, parked by the barn. Far away in the house a man was singing. It sounded like a spiritual.

14
The Inventor

"Damn lightning!"

Cred Faiging's tongue still smoldered with that coppery taste of flash fear—a nearby lightning strike, perhaps a death blow to the aging oak on the hilltop. He threw a pair of needle-nosed pliers onto the workbench and backed away from the electrical contraption he was building. It was an instinctive motion, animalistic and (he admitted to himself) entirely too late had there been any real danger. It was absurd, too, considering the sophisticated web of lightning rods protecting the five acres of compound. No man understood the mysteries of electricity like Cred Faiging, and he was determined it would not get the better of him.

Kim pushed through the plywood spring-door to the workshop, her odor preceding her by several yards. Her denims hugged across bony hips and the holster and bandolier crisscrossing her shoulders clicked softly as she shuffled to the bench to study Faiging's progress.

"Taking a break, yes?" she asked, oblivious of the new storm. "What's it this time? Torturing more plant fibers with the electrodes?" Mounted on the bench was a foot-long, tight coil of metal tubing valved to a freon cannister, a treasure he had bought for a few centimes from ignorant salvagers. Around the tubing wound a second coil, this one of electrical wire.

"No," replied the sallow inventor. He swept back his thinning hair, feeling his nerves shake down to normal. He sighed. "No fibers today. I've about run dry of permutations until I get some new plant buggers. This construction . . . well, I was wondering about the effect of sharp changes of temperature on magnetic fields."

Kim clucked and rolled a tobacco wad off her tongue into her left cheek. "Electromagnetism! Huh—dat legal this year?"

"Oh, bugger me," Faiging said, joining her mocking tone. "Bugger me up the canal if I should ever invoke a force of nature declared illegal or nonexistent!" He retrieved the pliers and dispensed with the jest. "You member the April contract, don't you? A dozen sump pumps for some Southland project—a dozen electric motors, ordered up by the Government. Guess that makes 'em legal—no?— legal till they're ordered undone again. Legal, legal, legal."

"Do ya idea that enough to keep the Inspectors packed away with their dynamite when they come round next? Ha. They'll have yer balls for brekkie."

"Huh. They need to keep my balls happy."

"There are a five or dozen dispatches you haven't opened even from last week," Kim admonished.

"I don't want to know yet. Let me finish."

"And a couple of trekkers are waiting down ta the gate. . . ."

"Poke 'em."

"Old one said to give the name Rosenthal Webb. A young one with him, soft 'n' nervous."

Faiging wore a sour look. "Ya don't gully the name Webb? A danger to talk to, if the Government hears of it. You've seen 'em, here onceta year maybe—usually for the warm stuff. Bangers, wire, out-region maps. Old poker. Missing a few pointers on his right hand, did ya see? Is it him?" Faiging held up a hand to demonstrate. The tops of his fingers were folded in, hidden, leaving four nubs.

Kim was scratching, bored. "I juss box the gear for 'em, I don' take their measurements."

"Well, let them in," Faiging said, "before the lightning Q's 'em. The young 'un wears a snap collar, or he stays outside. No talk."

Faiging worried over a dubiously soldered connection until Webb pushed through the door. The revolutionary's jumpsuit hung dirty and loose, like the skin of a boiled tomato. He wore a dark-colored backpack. His boots were muddy, hard leather, punctuated by canvas vents that were designed to lighten the weight and provide air to the feet.

Webb limped in, silently cursing the storm and its crippling humidity. "Gregory's coming in behind me," Webb said stonily, "and he ain't wearing a poking snap collar."

Faiging looked up.

"The snapper, thass too scary even for me," Webb said. "But Gregory's stripped clean. Kim agreed to that fast enough."

The young man entered, muscle-hard but pink-skinned naked and embarrassed. Kim loped in after him, mercifully pretending not to notice, and handed a supply list to Faiging.

The young man was anything but swaggering in his nudity. His shoulders hunched forward, bringing his arms into a frontward dangle that he hoped, futilely, might cover his crotch. "I'm . . . my name's Gregory. You're Mr. Faiging? The one what makes the generators and wenches . . . winches?" He blushed.

Faiging chuckled, amused that this was the sideman he had been so wary of. "I am Cred Faiging, yes," he said politely. "And, well, I designed those things and many more. It's the mountain grunts that actually *make* them now—out in the assembly houses. You could say that the trade we take from those frees me to play at more interesting pursuits."

The old inventor-trader recognized the wide-eyed awe of a fan. He poked his pliers in the direction of the newly formed tubing on the bench. "Now, it sounds that you was brought up right—with Faiging machinery about ya, no?"

"Plumb right, Mister," Gregory replied eagerly, and Webb winced that his assistant could be so easily toyed with. "I grew up on the saying 'If it ain't Faiging, don't trust your life to it.' "

Faiging nodded reverently—he had heard the same hundreds of times and never tired of it. The inventor returned to his new experiment, snipping the questionable solder connection apart and starting it anew.

"Son, it's juss the way of progress, thass all," Faiging said, eyes on his project. "Since the dawn of man—" He stopped himself. "Well, since the Big War, anyway, it's juss been the way of the world. Some rad-scarred salvager will find a rusted piece of ancient junk an' haul it in and sell it to an inventor, scientist, repairman, artist—call us anything you want."

Faiging waved his pliers grandly. "Thass the way the modern world was built. Reconstructed wire by wire, gear by gear—by myself and a handful of the like-minded."

Webb was growing impatient. "I have a supply list, and a tanker van to fill," he said.

Faiging did not look up. "Kim can take care of all that, as you know," he mumbled. "Why is it for once you cannot take supply quietly and pass on to do your maiming? Ya must parade into the main shop so that all know Cred Faiging supplies the enemies of the Government? Every time it's this way!"

Webb snorted. "You're a trader," he said, "a trader of all things and a player of all sides. And any customer you have is plumby enough to know that. Last I knew, you were no more a Government man than you were a fish peddler."

"That may be, but on touchy matters the Monitor is not much for forgiving."

"I'm headed out again," Webb said seriously, "into a thick bollocks I don't gully to the bottom. But on the edges of everything, is this odd bugger—a man you connected me with a year ago."

Faiging nodded. "Pec-Pec, the magic man. Don't hope to gully that one. You trade your nasty secrets with a bugger like that, now you're part of his crazy world—a story writ by a madman."

"Your machinery is solid," Webb said, "and that I trust

with my life, as they say. Your odd friends I don't. I have to know more."

Faiging paused with thought, then regarded the shivering young Gregory. He said to Kim, "The buster needs a covering. Bring 'im a blanket—not his gear, gully, just a blanket. One of *our* blankets." When Kim returned, Gregory settled onto a stool with the wool covering about him, more thankful to be able to cover his nakedness than to ward off the chill.

Faiging began with a slow but impatient air, as if addressing dull schoolchildren. "I want to make a test of something," the inventor said, "and mayhap you will see my point. Now, Gregory, answer me this: Who is the Monitor?"

The young man glanced to Webb, his brow wrinkling. "Who? The Monitor?"

Faiging was steadfast in his patience. "Just say what you truly believe," Faiging said flatly. "Tell me like I was just born—who is the Monitor, what does he do, where is he, and what does he look like?"

"Aww, nobody gots the whole of it, so what's the point?"

The old man put a foot on the lowest rung of Gregory's stool. "If you made your best guess, then," Faiging pressed on. "If you had to say the likest thing, what would it be?"

"I'd say the obvious, what ain't left to speculation. . . ."

"Which is?"

"Which is . . ." Gregory sighed. "The Monitor runs the Government, which is based in New Chicago. The Monitor probably lives there himself, by reason, and things operate rather smoothly—you're housed, get a roof and work and all—until one day you're informed by some pig-poking Lunch Minister or some such that cod guts are a delicacy and will be eaten raw at midday until supplies run out. . . ."

"The Monitor?"

"The Monitor," Gregory repeated, willing to be led back to the subject, away from his tirade. "He is a large, old mutated man. Secretive. The schoolchild tale is that he has three heads, heads like a dog or a bull, and lives in a hole in the ground, afraid of the light. Grew up in a science library, or some such.''

Faiging held up a hand, signaling for Gregory to stop. He motioned to Webb, saying, ''Your turn. The Monitor—whatever you truly believe.''

Webb's eyes darted to the window. Despite the storm, he clearly wanted to leave and be on the road. ''This is stupid,'' Webb said. ''So little is really known about the Monitor and what's to be had is probably more myth than fact. But for my part don't believe the Monitor's in New Chicago—haven't thought that for years—and he's not an individual, but a consortium of bungholes holed up far from the city. Three separate, normal individuals maybe, thus the three-headed tale.''

Faiging leaned contentedly into his workbench. ''Yes,'' he said, ''the point is that all those with the true gut-ball information are either in power or dead. The Monitor could be anything from a three-headed monster in New Chicago to a paranoid committee that relocates itself every few months in the countryside.''

''I was asking you about Pec-Pec,'' said Webb.

''And I was illustrating just that,'' replied Faiging. ''No one *knows* anything about Pec-Pec just like no one *knows* anything about the Monitor. The Monitor runs a government that has precise rules, and those who do not obey die or disappear. Pec-Pec—he cannot be found either. He cannot be described accurately, and his existence is just a matter of faith. He is known as a gentleman, a statesman, a magician, and a thief. Probably there are four or five Pec-Pecs as well. The one I introduced you to, I just cannot be responsible for. Gully? If he leads you to disaster with one of his fantasies, don't come bombing my compound in revenge. I just introduced you once. Now, I've tried to warn ya away.''

''We wouldn't bomb you, Mr. Faiging,'' Gregory said innocently. ''The committee's ordered a peaceful mission—no bangers. It wouldn't have let us come, otherwise.''

Faiging's smile twisted, and he held up the order sheet Kim had passed to him. ''Then ya haven't seen your boss's supply list, have ya, boy?''

15
Rutherford Cross

There was not much about old Rutherford Cross that his neighbors agreed on. But this much no one would dispute: He owned eighty acres of land on the outskirts of Kingstree in the Sector that was called back then South Carolina. The earth was rich enough (although a might sandy), but he farmed only a small patch measuring eight rows by a hundred feet—corn, cabbage, rutabagas, string beans. He had no teeth—had never had any in anyone's memory— and his leathery face resembled a collapsing jack-o- lantern. Not a trace of paint remained on his shack, which stood among towering oaks hung with Spanish moss in the center of his property. Most neighbors speculated that he owned so much land just so that no one would have any business coming near him.

Grammy Baker, who had never lived more than a couple of miles from Cross, swore that he had looked precisely the same when she was a little girl 70-odd years before. It was even gossiped that he was 250 years old and had come from Africa himself on a slave boat—a notion that the younger folks poo-pooed, of course.

Sam Weathers, who delivered dry goods to Cross's house on the first of each month (unless it fell on a Sunday), had heard Cross say once that he was on his seventh wife—Lydia—and the courthouse records did show four legal marriages under his name, the first one being to Melissa Bailey in 1904.

Children? Strangely, nobody quite knew, but skeptics reckoned that there had been two Rutherford Crosses, father and son, and that the distinction between the two had blurred—thus accounting for his unnatural life span.

Cross was held in high esteem when it came to doctoring. He could set a broken bone, cure a fever, and had delivered dozens of babies with Lydia's help. The Clinic doctors, the kind with framed diplomas on the wall, would get pretty hot about that. But mention such things as "voodoo" or "mojo" or "medicine bag" to Cross and he was as likely as anyone to roll his eyes and spit out a spiteful *"Pshaw."*

The old gentleman also was known to have a substantial root cellar. Grammy Baker had once let on that Rutherford Cross had dug clear through the earth and had spent more time in China than Marco Polo. No one gave much credence to Grammy Baker.

It was in the year 2013 that Lydia got pregnant. She and Rutherford Cross stood solemnly on their front porch in the bone-chilling damp one night—her big-bellied, him permanently stooped. Their eyes took in the sky. It was turned a broiling red by those magnificent bombs that were slapping the landscape with nuclear fire.

"Lydia, you go on down ta root cellar an' don't come up," Cross said. He settled into a rocking chair on the porch. "Me, I'm gonna rest these ol' bones now."

Lydia did go to the root cellar. She lived by lantern light and subsisted on smoked hams and shelf after shelf of canned vegetables set up by Cross himself. Above, a year-long wind storm was raging, and in the middle of what should have been a steamy summer Lydia delivered her own child. She named the boy Rutherford Cross but later found herself calling him Pec-Pec, baby talk for the youngster's favorite food, pickles.

16
The Valve Job

A car horn honked outside and Seth Graham dropped the roasted chicken breast to his plate—"Damn!"—and went to the window, licking grease from his fingers. There were a jeep and a van below. A young fellow in a Government jumpsuit stood in the gravel waving a small clipboard at him in the rain.

Deedee Graham swallowed a spoonful of baked potato and said, "They can fend for themselves, can't they Sethy? Can't they see we're shut down for the night?"

"Ya'd think so, Deedee. Ya'd think so. But if it's an emergency . . ." Graham took the keys from a nail on the wall. He slipped his feet into his galoshes, not bothering to buckle them, pulled his slicker from the hanger on the door, and went out. The living quarters were raised on stilts well above the flood level of River 011, and the area below the house had been enclosed to form a garage. Graham wearily thumped down the wet wooden steps.

The man in the jumpsuit had curly blond hair plastered to his forehead. "Is this the East Saint Louis Fuel Depot?"

he asked, shouting unnecessarily, as if Graham were deafened by the rain.

Graham turned to examine the two-foot-high lettering across the garage doors: E. ST. LOUIS FUEL DEPOT. He enjoyed the moment, in a way. "Reckon so," he said.

"I'm looking for Seth Graham."

"Well, you found him, an' he'd like to get back to his dinner directly," Graham said. "What can I do for ya?"

"My boss is in the jeep—Rosenthal Webb," the younger man said. He shielded his face with the clipboard.

Graham's eyebrows rose. "Can't place the name. Sorry."

"Well, we think we've got a cracked cylinder. Not much time to spare, either."

"I'll speak to your Mr. Webb," Graham said, "but this is mighty peculiar. You folks *are* Supply drivers, aren't you? We don't handle any private business."

Graham slogged over to the farther vehicle and opened its canvas and plastic door. A graying man sat in the driver's seat. It was a weather-worn face bristling with silver beard stubble, and the skin under his chin was beginning to sag. The back compartment of the jeep, Graham noted, was piled high with equipment cases and outdoor gear. The aging man had his hands on the steering wheel, and the four fingers of his right hand were shorn in half.

"Lot of nerve," Graham said.

"I didn't plan this," Webb responded.

"Well, why don't you just steal a new pig-pokin' jeep," Graham said. He pulled at his mustache and looked up and down the dark highway. "Don't say you don't know how."

"Can't afford to risk the hoopla. I've got a long way to go and I need to go quietly."

"Cracked cylinder? Well, hmmm, ya gotta lift the engine, pull off the heads, grind the valves, replace that cylinder. . . . Ya didn't say ya was in a hurry did ya?"

"Matter of fact," Webb said, grinning, "I'm in a hurry, too."

Graham rubbed his forehead, ignoring the rivulets of rain trickling between his fingers. "You know how this depot has built up? There's never fewer than thirty, forty Government types around. All day and night I drink and piss Government now. And you come roll in, devil-may-care. I was startin' to think I'd never see you again. Now ya bring this boy around." He jabbed a finger toward the van. "Now he'll still be dropping by here twenty years after you die. Damn!"

Graham unlocked the double garage doors, waved both vehicles in, and disappeared into the blackness outside. It was a roomy garage, with two pits and two hydraulic lifts, designed to serve a high-traffic crossroads of Government supply routes. Five autos could be under repair at the same time. Webb eased his jeep under a block-and-tackle rig and killed the engine, then strode to the van.

"Where did he go, Gregory?"

"I don't know. Kind of cranky, isn't he?"

"He was born cranky."

A pair of headlights appeared at the garage entrance, spotlighting the two men. Gregory fell flat against the driver's seat and Webb moved to the shielded side of the van. The headlights crept in, and Webb saw that it was a late model Government jeep, with Graham at the wheel. He parked beside the other jeep, walked to the garage doors, and pulled them closed.

"Help yourself to the tools, fellas," Graham said. "Just put 'em back and put 'em back clean."

Gregory's pulse was still racing, but he slumped out of the van and made a quick survey of the tools racked against the back wall. "Well, I can do the job," he said, "but I don't know that the second jeep is what we need. Just having the new parts would move things along faster. A place this big would have to have a parts house."

Graham frowned. He glared at Gregory in disbelief, then at Webb, and back again. "Ya don't have to *fix* anything, boy. Like you say, no time. Just *switch the engines*. Shee! The Government jeep has to be out back again by five A.M., and when it heads out, well"—he shrugged—"so the guy blew a cylinder."

Upstairs, Graham returned to his supper. Deedee Graham's quizzical expression asked the question.

"Deedee . . ." He stared down at the cooling chicken breast. "It's Rosenthal. Rosenthal Webb."

"Land-o-gosh, I've got to go give him a big kiss!"

"No!"

Deedee was hurt by his tone. "You love that man as much as I do, Sethy," she said, voice quavering.

"He's in a hurry," Seth Graham said, "and the less we act like we know him the better off we'll be."

Deedee's eyes welled up with tears.

As day broke, the van and the jeep pulled to the side of a little-used road near the banks of the wide, glistening River 011. Webb ran up to the van, and Gregory already had the map out.

"We shouldn't try to cross here," Webb said. "We'll find a ferry or bridge, oh, a hunnerd miles up the river, around here." He poked at the map.

"Hannibal."

Webb smiled. "Just us and our elephants."

"Elephants?"

"An old myth. I'll tell you about it sometime."

It was then that Gregory saw over Webb's shoulder an astoundingly improbable structure. Planted on the opposite riverbank stood a lone arch, hundreds of feet high. It was made of shiny metal, which threw off tiny flashes of the rising sun. Webb noted Gregory's gape and turned.

"One of the wonders of the old world," Webb said. He laughed, and rested an elbow on the van's window frame.

"What is it?"

"An arch. Uh, it's supposed to be something of a mystery, but it must have been built for some reason."

"Ya know," said Gregory, "looking at it, ya'd think the entire world were a tree ornament and that this is where it's hung from."

"Folks say, mostly, that it was some kind of carnival ride. There's a little chamber inside that took people up and down. Doesn't work anymore, of course."

"So, what was that place over there?"

"Well, West Saint Louis, I imagine. An amusement park?"

17
Two Government Guests

Moberly felt ill. One of the two new late arrivals was a double assault on the senses, and the most quickly identifiable offense was that perfume. It angered her; it was as if the fellow had entered the inn's dining room and had swatted every person present on the nose. This was the reek of New Chicago, of course.

Visually he was a perversity as well. It was a sickly styling that Moberly considered the product of a frenetic fashionableness. Removed from his urban context the man appeared awkward and clownlike. (Moberly thought, somehow, of a hairless moose wearing a negligee.) That ludicrous hair-handle sprouted from the left side of his head like a wayward antenna, and Moberly, smiling now as she greeted the men, remembered the tale Anton Takk had just told her about the scuffle in his New Chicago hotel room.

The newcomer humorlessly exhibited his Security credentials, traded in his Government chit, and signed the register, booking separate rooms for himself and the older, more reasonably dressed gentleman who followed obediently in his shadow.

Takk had asked to hear of any Government arrivals, and Moberly would see to that soon, she told herself. But for now, she must deal with a Supply driver dozing on a dinner table. He was a Supply man of the old school—hard driving, hard-drinking—and at the moment his nose was pressed firmly into a yellowing tablecloth. One inopportune roll of his body could wipe out a dozen empty ale bottles—containers that Moberly had hoped to refill in her brewing operation in the barn. And then there was the kitchen to shut down, the leftovers to pack away for the next night. Moberly sighed and rounded the counter, hoping she wouldn't have to drag the driver's dead weight to his room. (She hoped, too, that he wouldn't start singing again.) Wouldn't you know that out of seven customers tonight *this* guy would be the one with a room upstairs?

She remembered that she had not given the new customers directions to their rooms, but they were gone, apparently willing to find their own way.

"Couldn't we leave your detective work till the morning?" complained Gould Papier. There was a ring of dark wetness around the bottom of his tunic. Having learned his lesson, Papier hitched it up clear of the puddles in the Moberly Inn's parking lot. At least the rain has stopped, he considered. Kerbaugh would have us out here getting drenched.

"Humor me," said Kerbaugh, and Papier pondered the irony of the expression. The Inspector had no humor.

"There's nothing to *see* unless we get a lantern. I'll get the one in our jeep," Papier said, picking his way across the gravel toward the barn.

"Your eyes will adjust quickly. If he's here, I'd rather not draw attention with a light."

"Here?" said Papier. "But I checked all of these license plates"—he gestured at the row of vehicles—"and you examined the guest registry. . . ."

Kerbaugh came to an abrupt halt at the back of one of the Supply trucks. He studied in silence, then marched to the truck's cab, peered inside, and returned. The muscles in his jaw were alternately flexing and relaxing, like a heart-beat.

"Mr. Papier, use your powers of perception—still developing, though they may be—and tell me what is unusual about this truck."

It was a frustratingly ordinary truck—once white, now dented and rusted and mud-caked to an uneven beige. The tires were the knobby standard issue, the side mirror was cracked but serviceable, the back lock was . . . was that it?

"Well, the lock isn't the normal slide-bolt assembly. I think that's what they call it. The driver must have lost it and threaded a chain through the handles."

Kerbaugh smiled coldly. "Good. But yes, it could be that one of your noble drivers is just improvising. No doubt he was generous enough to buy a lock out of his own wallet to protect a Government shipment. And it was probably that upstanding specimen we just saw in the dining room, don't you think?"

"I'll be sure to get his name," Papier said.

Kerbaugh snorted. "Now, what else? How about this license plate you copied the numbers off of—the ones that don't match those of the stolen truck?" The Security man scraped his foot across a corner of the plate, and there was a short twang of vibrating metal.

Papier knelt and squinted in the darkness, and the back of his tunic settled into the mud. "Hmn. Looks like a piece of an old plate under the current one."

"And why is that odd?" asked Kerbaugh triumphantly.

"Well, the plates on these trucks are permanent, of course. They're never removed until the truck is scrapped."

Kerbaugh clamped an arm around Papier's shoulder and walked him to the center of the parking lot. "And now look around you," the Inspector said in a boyish, confidential tone. "The barn, the trucks, that collapsing clot of shacks this Moberly calls an inn. Do you see it all in a different light now? As if the moon had come from behind the clouds and illuminated the secrets here? All of this from tiny scraps of evidence!"

Then Kerbaugh laughed aloud, too loud, and Papier decided the man was quite mad.

Code: A02–33 Kerbaugh
Destination: Monitor/Eyes only
Routing: SATline II/Scramble
Origin: Moberly Inn wireless/Linex 44–E87
Message: Subject on premises. Continuing site inspec-
       tion per SOP.

Moberly's days were regimented, something essential to the lone proprietor of an inn. The front desk duties, the kitchen work, the guest-room upkeep, and auxiliary proj-ects, such as gardening, ale-making, and raising chickens, demanded order and structure. Fortunately, her body re-quired only five hours of sleep a night, midnight to 5:00 A.M., but she needed the total darkness of her basement living quarters to accomplish satisfactory sleep. Her only discretionary time came in the afternoons—if there were no customers to attend to.

Moberly had carved the bedroom out of the southwest corner of the original farmhouse's basement. It had a low ceiling—she had built a new hardwood floor for it two feet above the basement floor concrete as protection from oc-casional seepage. At 5 feet, 5 inches, Moberly was in no danger of bumping her head; Anton Takk, she told herself, would have a problem down here. From outside the room it looked like, perhaps, a tool shed or a furnace room: walls of bare studs laced with cobwebs.

Inside, Moberly had lined the walls with rough barn siding and fashioned a closet with sliding doors. The only free-standing furniture was a dresser recently appropriated from a guest room. The bed consisted of a springless mattress on a platform built up from the floor; a shelf nailed to one wall served as a nightstand. An electric lamp with a small, torn shade burned on the nightstand, evidence of the electric wiring in the main house that the newer additions did not have.

Here was Moberly's rebellion against regimentation. The blankets and sheets lay in a rolling tangle across the bed, and they were never "made" in the way that Moberly straightened the guest room covers daily. She preferred to have her own bed like this, in the way that some people feel most comfortable with a cluttered desk or kitchen.

Moberly unlaced her boots and pulled off her sweater and trousers, which she folded perfunctorily and pushed into cubbyholes in the closet. In bed, she drew the chaos of covers over herself like a child hiding in a pile of leaves. She flipped the light off. Would this be a restless night? She feared it would be. First Anton Takk; then two Security men; now the inn was silent and Takk was not in his room. His truck was still here—where could *he* be?

She must have been dozing, finally—although it was hard be sure—when she started awake with a sharp fright. There had been a sound, loud, and Moberly had to think frantically in the darkness to identify it—a creaking snap, metal on wood. Then she knew: nails being yanked out of a board.

Even in absolute darkness, Moberly could study the basement—a precise mental image of it, anyway—for the possible sources of the sound. She had barred the door at the top of the stairs with a two-by-four set into brackets, which meant that she was alone in the basement. And the sound could only have come from a floorboard above being pried loose, from one of the high windows she had shuttered over to block out light, or from the door itself.

And then she heard the two-by-four clatter down the stairs, which settled the matter. Moberly left the bed and found her clothes by feel, instinctively avoiding the spots in the floor that creaked. From the bedroom door she watched the staircase as she dressed. The door at the top opened and closed again. Someone was descending, and Moberly reviewed the possibilities: Takk? But why would he break in the door? The drunken Supply driver? It was doubtful *he'd* be up and around already. Thieves? The Security men?

And then Moberly sat on the step-up to her bedroom, knowing the answer. She felt not so much fear as a deep, deep sadness. Violated, raped in an abstract way. She pictured the house, the barn, the grounds—the framework of an independent life suddenly under Government scrutiny. And coming to a terribly swift end. In past years the notion of repentance had passed through her mind—quickly, actually never seriously considered. Who could really live such a gray life? Who could subsist? Moberly waited for the welling up of regret, and it did not come. But her life was ending.

"Now will you light the lantern?" hissed a male voice.

A match was struck, a lamp lit, and there in the blinding light were the Security men: Kerbaugh, his pale bald head large and moonlike against the blackness; Papier fidgeting under a fresh tunic, another drab ankle-brushing outfit with a wide belt at the waist.

"It's a museum down here," Papier said, casting his widening eyes over the large open room, "even more than the back room upstairs!" And it was true. The basement floor was an orchard of tired machinery situated in neat rows to allow orderly passage. They were hulking, black contraptions with forgotten uses from forgotten decades, some of them covered with oily sheeting, others heavily greased, and still others hopeless and rusting their way into oblivion.

Kerbaugh wagged a finger toward the northward darkness and said, "We'll start at that end. I want to check every one of these ... things." He headed up a corridor in the center of the floor and Papier followed, apprehensive about leaving the security of the stairway but also amused to watch Kerbaugh clutch his white tunic to his thighs, away from the grimy monstrosities on either side. The lantern, against the procession of braces and frames and wingnuts and humps and muscley springs, sent macabre shadow forms marching in the opposite direction down the stone walls on either side. Papier longed for his tidy office in New Chicago.

Near the north wall the collection of machinery ended, and the two investigators entered a clear area of flooring. Before them stood one last massive black sculpturework of metal, shrouded in white sheeting and resembling a theatrical dragon paraded down the streets by children on holidays. Kerbaugh set the lantern on the concrete and strode to one end of the machine. He grabbed a corner of the sheeting and pulled slowly, turning one forearm over the other and letting the drape roll up into a bundle.

A sinister black steel skeleton was revealed, an apparatus dominated by five consecutive upright braces. There were giant wheels on each side used for manual operation. In the guts of the hardware were cylinder rollers and inky beds of lead inscribed in bas relief with illegible markings.

"This," announced Kerbaugh, "is a printing press!"

Papier was stunned. It was obviously true. All about lay the implements of printing: barrels of ink, shelves of paper in varying sizes, thicknesses, and colors, and a long counter stocked with pens and ink bottles and magnifying glasses and straight-edges and dozens of Government forms—or careful copies of them. Papier was amused by his own tinge of sadness—well, the assemblage *was* a monument to an individual's ingenuity—and he wondered how the handsome machine would meet its end. By sledgehammer? They had brought no dynamite—this wasn't *that* kind of Government expedition.

When Kerbaugh returned to the lantern he exploded with profanities: "Well if this ain't a roll in the shit!" He was staring with disbelief at the front of his tunic, which was spattered with dozens of oily spots. He rubbed the damaged fabric between his fingers.

Papier approached the lantern to inspect his own clothing but there was nothing to see in the dark material. At that moment, though, he felt a droplet hit his face and a sting spread through his left eye. He rubbed at the eye socket, spat on his hand, and rubbed again. When the pain subsided, Papier grasped the lantern by the overhandle and lifted the light high. He squinted, and an examination of the ceiling confirmed his suspicion: Droplets of a clear liquid, probably turpentine, kerosene, or gasoline—he could smell it now— were falling rapidly from the rafters.

Kerbaugh seemed transfixed by the shower. "Papier," he intoned, "directly above us is the dining room. Someone has spilled fuel over the floor. A *lot* of fuel. We must go up and have a look."

It was then that the scent of woodsmoke hit Papier's nostrils, and he obediently bolted south down the corridor with the lantern. He was near the foot of the stairs when Kerbaugh halted him with a shrill cry: "Don't . . . leave me . . . in . . . the *dark!*"

Papier turned and held the lantern high to show him the

way. Kerbaugh stood motionless in the spot where Papier had left him, a quivering toadstool beside the black press. Abruptly, the entire front of Kerbaugh's tunic turned gray, and a river of liquid gushed down his right leg. Deciding that Kerbaugh was not going to follow, Papier turned again and bounded up the stairs. The wooden steps were sopping with flammable liquid, and when he crashed against the door at the top his fears were confirmed: It had been locked by key from the outside and, it seemed from the impact, there was a heavy object against it.

For a moment Papier thought a burst of herculean strength might open the way, but reason intervened, and he splashed down the steps wondering what ideas Kerbaugh might have. He saw no flames yet, but the smoke was getting awfully thick.

18
The Lovers

Dear Moberly,

When I script these words they are no less painful for being able to look at them. You'd think me quite the pig poker for leaving you with just writings, but I fear that my tongue would never make it through the explaining that needs doing—why I am gone by the time that you read this.

I can see now that for me to stay any longer would mean disaster for us both, and to once again be the destruction of a loved one, well, the guilt would kill.

I did say "once again." Some of the story I told ya, about the letter I shipped around asking for money and maps, and how it all arrived as in a fairy tale. Hoo. I told ya not all of why I wanted to run.

There was a woman arrived more than a year ago in Camp Blade, woman I had thought to wed named Nora Londi. Midday break each day, we would push up through the forest on the hill above town—the best place from which to spot wanderers. We would scatter our shirts and trousers enough to make an appreciable blanket. And then once exhausted on the spread—sorry, but I want you to know all of this tale—she would tell me the stories of her journey.

In that, she was like many who passed through the camp. Beaten people, weathered by working their way across the country. But really stronger for the effort. And I envy their experience, me never having left Camp Blade. They all have stories, ya, and it was Nora Londi what told me one of the most curious.

Five years ago, she tells me, she was working Sector 1— a farming outpost called New Bern—barning on a tobacco farm. (I gully that's where she got so fond of good smoke.) She was hefting in the curing barn, which was racked through with cross beams. She would have to monkey up the cross beams to the top, hang a stick load of tobacco leaves, and then climb back down for the next one. That until the barn's full. The leaves would drip juice on her, she'd tell me, until she looked like a slug at the end of the day.

So third day out, all the guys at the barn are looking at her funny. Supposed to be one person on the barn floor handing her racks of tobacco leaves, but there's five of 'em this morning, most of the guys just kicking dust while one or two works. Then there's eight of 'em, and then about twenty, and then she gave up on hanging tobacco—something was up.

In comes this big ol' pig woman named Pawga—she's the mule boss at the stable, almost wider than she was tall. Nora could hear her breathing from the top of the barn. And the guys start yellin', and the money comes out, and she'd seen this all before—it was a dog fight, only she was one of the dogs, her and Pawga. She wasn't meant to win this one, either. Nothing was on her side—not weight, not the betting, not the foreknowin' of the fight.

So she just dived from the cross beams and hit the dirt, rolling toward the corner where there was some old tools. She goes pushing through this rusty junk till she finds a cloth bag the size of a brick, and it tears away like nothing, it's so old. And inside, damn if it isn't a rusty log chain like they use for tractor hauling.

This woman Nora is a muscler, y'unnerstand. She takes the log chain an' starts spinning it over her head, then *letting out a little more, and a little more, and the tip end is movin' pretty fast, like a buzz saw. Then she steps forward and, well, she never did want to do Pawga any harm. She probably didn't want the fight any more than Nora did. The guys were the ones what wanted to see a fight.*

Hoo. Well, bear-busting with such a story, this is where I start to go wrong. When it's lights out at Camp Blade all are asleep, or at least staring from their bunks at the ceilings. But for some of us these rules were flexible—for the Badgers, and for those of us with access to goods traded on the black market. Those people being Supply drivers or warehousers such as myself who know how to rework bills of lading.

We had built a hideaway in the heart of the warehouse, a cramped little room created by the careful stacking of shipping crates. It was protected by a maze of outer walkways that could be shifted or obliterated in a moment by a forklift driver.

So this night I get piss drunk on ale, beard-sopping laid out in our after-hours den. And I tell Nora Londi's story, I couldn't help it, leaning on a couple of crates I tell the guys the all of it.

Oh, they hooted so much they were snorting ale foam out their noses, all but Sgt. Krieger. He was kind of quiet and sober through the telling.

And the next day I learn the why of that: The pig poker jails her for the killings, hoping he'd gain a stripe for it.

That's when I went gullybonkers and wrote the letters, sending them out in supply shipments. I did lie a bit in the letters, but there were friends to protect, and I needed the extra measure of sympathy or no outsider would have thrown assistance, do you think?

The night I was ready to leave I pounded Sgt. Krieger in his bed with the backside of a logger axe. The Badgers've got to know it was me, so the telling of it makes no difference now. I pounded Sgt. Krieger until ya couldn't tell him from the mattress.

—Anton

19
Above the Village

Nora Londi squinted at the circle of light in the ceiling of her cell. There was a familiar "friend" at the rooftop door: her hat. It hovered there, a brown fedora, a little misshapen and discolored from its recent drenching. As her eyes adjusted, she understood—it was wobbling atop Loo's tiny head.

Loo shoved the rope ladder through the hole, and it bounced and settled into a herky-jerky swing that caught the attention of the llama Diego and his two compadres.

Loo called down, "Oo-oo. Oo-onga." And Diego replied, "Hoorma. Hoong." Slowly he turned his dignified gaze to Londi. "Go . . . up," he said.

Londi climbed the ladder into a blinding, arid whiteness. As she stood stunned in the outside air for the first time in a week, Loo pulled up the rope ladder and stuffed it into a canvas satchel. Londi took her hat from Loo's head as the wiry little woman worked. Londi was unsure whether she would be allowed to keep it. How much of a prisoner was she? She glanced inside the hat, then slapped it against her thigh, flipped the hat onto her head, and pulled the brim low to shield the sunlight.

Loo seemed not to notice. She wrinkled her nose at the stench of excrement wafting from below. In manic movements, she unlaced the leather ties on a second sack and withdrew a sling, a large Cred Faiging pulley-and-tripod assembly that fit over the door-hole in the ground. A hand crank was bolted to the side of the tripod. In a few minutes Diego had been winched to the surface, and he stamped and harumphed in the bright midday.

Something was about to happen, something in this peculiar little village had been decided, and Londi and Diego were edgy.

From under the hat brim, Londi studied the canyon. There was the waterfall to the east that she had heard thundering for days. She had only seen the far edge of it through the little circular windows. Now she took in the whole of it—an awesome white fist pounding the turbine. Far to the west the lake grew mirrorlike, reflecting the shocking blue sky and red-brown rock walls dotted with a scattering of scrubby trees. It was a stark and unnatural juxtaposition, this meeting of sheer canyon and manmade lake. Surely, underwater the vertical walls continued their plunge; the lake had to be hundreds of feet deep. Just below there was sandy embankment, a beach—and that probably was manmade as well.

In her days underground, Londi had envisioned more of a bustling village around her, a small hillside metropolis. But there was little to see. A chicken cackled by. To the west there were a few whisps of smoke rising from disguised chimneys. Occasionally a dark naked figure would appear among the rocks and melt into the shadows again. There *had* to be other structures dotted about the rocky slope, but from this vantage point they were either not visible or were well camouflaged.

Londi judged the narrow lake to be a hundred feet below, and then thought it might be five hundred feet. It was disorienting not having a familiar object down there by which to judge the scale. It was the same gazing upward. That vegetation at the canyon rim—were they pygmy shrubs, or a stand of giant spruces? Londi felt dizzy.

Loo clutched the hair on each side of Diego's neck, murmured into his ear, then leaped onto his back. A set of long, folded wings dangled from her right shoulder by a strap. Londi noted that Loo had left the tripod in place, as if it would be needed again, and she deduced that they would be returning "home" eventually. That is, at least Diego would return; the rope ladder *she* had used had been bagged up.

As she steered Diego up the gorge wall, Loo could not resist running her fingers through the llama's soft fur.

"Hey, Diego," Londi called ahead, "maybe she thinks you'd make a nice rug."

The large beast stopped in midstride and turned his head, right front paw still poised in the air. "No," the animal managed to say after much thought. "Hoom. You . . . go in soup."

There. So Diego was as cranky as she was. But Londi was feeling better in the sunlight, fresh air, walking again.

At times the path meandered in an obliging gradual ascent, but more often it rose alarmingly straight up the rocky wall. Londi found the gravelly ground unpredictable under her hiking boots, the loose pebbles sliding too easily. She paced herself in short and careful strides, which was just as well, the breathing being more difficult at this altitude.

An hour into the climb, the trio scrambled up onto an outcropping that allowed an overview of the village below, and Londi was astounded at the elaborate layout. Like her cell, the several dozen structures scattered about the hillside were built in natural-looking, sloping formations, their walls made up of indigenous rock. From a great distance, she knew, they would be invisible.

As the sun moved across the sky, Londi trudged upward, staring into the llama's hindquarters. She grew to envy the animal's precise, unerring paces. She also envied Loo's leisurely ride, but Londi knew she herself would be too heavy for a llama on this terrain, even for a brute the size of Diego. She sweated heavily into her shirt and the sweat burned away quickly in the dry air. A steady breeze began drifting up from below, which seemed to make Loo restless—she was turning, looking down, then toward the sky and the canyon rims, and down again.

Londi was in such a daze—her mind fixed on thirst, her vision now crisscrossed with hallucinated shooting stars—that when the group stopped, it all seemed so absurd. Loo dismounted; Diego quietly sat back on his haunches. Let's go, Londi wanted to say, up the canyon! But she was incapable of speech. Her throat felt so dry and crackly that it might bleed.

And then her exasperation began to fade. Slowly she realized that they had arrived at their destination, a dangerously sloping ledge little wider than the trail itself. There was an opening in the rock here, a cave entrance in the shape of a sagging triangle, and Loo disappeared into it. Londi turned and gazed down into the gaping gorge to test her theory and, yes, the village below had vanished.

Diego interrupted her concentration, nudging his wet snout into the back of her hand. "No . . . way out," he said. It was a plaintive voice, as if he were worrying about her thoughts.

Londi wiped her nose. "Hoo. *You* bounce up a mountain without thinkin'—instinct. Me, I suck in the territory. Gotta look around, map it out. Instinct."

When Loo returned she looked dispirited and afraid. The fingers of her left and right hands were intertwined and pressed into her crotch. She watched the cave apprehensively.

And then the figure emerged. He stood seven feet tall, humped and husky, a grotesque assemblage of flesh. The man brought a musky scent into the odorless outdoors. It was a muscley body, yet unattractive. The skin was an astonishing, blinding white.

Londi riveted on the face: He had a protruding, bovine jaw topped by a long flat nose with tear-shaped nostrils. Propped on that nose was a pair of sunglasses with mirrored lenses reflecting twin vistas of the canyon below. His head darted left and right hyperactively, and wild Nordic-yellow hair surrounded a pair of tiny horns protruding from the top of his head. He was naked, and a large scrotum waggled between his legs, dwarfing his little nub of a penis.

"Hello," came a throaty voice. While Loo quivered, Diego stared meditatively into the gorge, pretending disinterest.

Londi found words, and they seemed inept the moment they tumbled out: "Do you live here? Have we come to see you?"

"This is where I live," the monster rumbled. "And you are here at my invitation. I am your leader."

Londi decided she was being toyed with. Information came hard in this community, and it rankled her not knowing where she stood.

"You're not my leader," she ventured, remembering that she had snatched the red badge off of the inert body of Red Boss in the waterfall netting. "I'm a Government Transport deputy, and they'll be looking for me by now, I 'spect. Armed searchers, probably, from over there at Blue Hole."

The behemoth snorted and squinted toward the sky. "Do you play chess by any chance?" he asked. He did not wait for an answer, assuming it to be no. "You are check-mated, Nora Londi. I have you covered from all sides, no matter what you say or pretend. You, dear red lady, have stumbled upon a canyon that you may never leave, a canyon that I rule quite adamantly. Just ask Loo, here. There was once a little misunderstanding between us about decorum, wasn't there, Loo? And now you're missing your tongue."

Loo stared intently at her toes.

The hunched man cocked the left side of his face toward Londi, his two mirror-covered eyes being well separated by the protruding snout. He rubbed at his crotch and continued, "About that Government work of yours—well, we all know that ain't so, don't we? *Red Boss* was with the Government. *Was*.

"Red Boss's dead, ya know. We've got his head on a stake now, up by one of those trails above the waterfall. We really must discourage the inquisitive, and Red Boss is serving us this final duty. And as for the rest of him . . ."

The burly man thrust his belly forward and slapped it with a grimy palm.

But the giant's patience and good nature were dwindling.

Londi did not seem sufficiently staggered by his revelations. Even before his bizarre countenance, she seemed to be devoting more of her attention to the village below and the majesty of the surrounding gorge walls.

"Nora," he said, "I know that you are not Government because I *am* Government. Not just of this gorge—of all the Sectors, and eventually beyond. I am *the* Government. I *run* the Government."

"Then you're the Monitor," Londi murmured, resigned.

"Mmm. Wrong, wrong place, Nora—wrong stream to fall into, wrong waterfall, wrong canyon." She paused. "Ain't you supposed to have three heads?"

The beast scratched at his belly, squinted at the sun, then glanced at his quickly reddening forearm. "Humph. Now, won't you come inside?"

The monster ducked and disappeared into the triangular blackness. Loo stood still on the ledge, clearly assigned to bring up the rear.

Londi approached the mouth of the cave and cupped her hands around her mouth: "I do play chess," she shouted, "and have you taken into account the knights coming into play?" There was no response—just the flat blackness— and Londi had no assurance that the lie had landed home.

Loo then slapped Londi's rear, more forcefully than necessary, and Londi reluctantly crept into the black void.

Alone with Loo, Diego bore a puzzled look. "You . . . play chest?" Then he followed his companion into the rock wall.

20
Music Not Thrown

*"Music is the nearest expression of man's actual soul
and being. Do not taint it with impure thought."*
—From the writings of Rutherford Cross
Book III, Chapter IV.
Excerpted by permission of Ligkh Priest Lit Mannah,
34UH5.

Tha'Enton nearly fainted trying to purify his music this
night. He could not allow himself to think of these unknown
wanderers in the village and what they might mean. The
advocations chosen for him—Sound Maker and Defender—
had defined a spartan livelihood that promised many spiritual benefits were he to remain faithful to his task until
death. Now, more than ever, he must concentrate.

Out of all musical positions, being a bonesman required
the most dexterity. Some instruments were considered totally rhythmic, and others were much more melodic, but
being a bonesman required an intuitive facility at both. His
instrument was the Pa—a wood, leather, and cotton-fiber
assemblage measuring 5½ feet wide, surrounding him in

the shape of a concave quarter sphere. There were actually 718 instruments included in the Pa, 718 pairs of "bones" arranged in this rack surrounding Tha'Enton. Each set of bones consisted of two slightly curved pieces of ebony made to be rattled between the fingers. At precisely the right time, the bonesman was to pluck the proper set of bones from the rack, let them twitter or rumble in his hands (the size determined the tonal range), and then toss them back into their proper place with a carefully aimed flick.

The confident and showy bonesmen lately had taken up a sport that enraptured the more knowledgeable among the spectators: During the course of an evening's play, such musicians would toss a set of bones aside when they had thocked out their final tones for the evening, instead of returning them to the rack, where they could be safely retrieved. The trick lay in having the foreknowledge of when during the night's repertoire each of the 718 sets of bones had become obsolete. To toss the ebony sounders aside prematurely, into a growing pile of the polished sticks, would mean musical disaster and months of shame for the musician. Not coincidentally, the musicians who reveled in the game of chess also tended to immerse themselves in the risky throwaway of bones.

Bone tossing was by no means a required activity, but still there were those in the milling audience who loudly expressed their disappointment that Tha'Enton was not attempting the feat this evening. (There was a small band of purists in the community, on the other hand, that argued that such throwing actually chipped the little ebonies occasionally and was therefore detrimental to the musical art. But a Sounder as brash as Tha'Enton could not suddenly claim to be among them.)

There would be no stick tossing tonight. Let them fibber, Tha'Enton told himself. I have a throb of foreknowing, and I mustn't be distracted.

So it was that the crowd pressing and shifting through the village Center for the evening's Sundown carried an edge of dissatisfaction. There was a dusty tussle or two, ending with the loser's limp body being dragged off to the pyres. The children swooped in to rub the blood into the dirt until it disappeared, thus hurrying the ghastly gorings into history.

And so it became a bad night musically, with Tha'Enton presiding over the uninspired soundings and the audience acutely aware of the shortcoming. The Pa's leathery aroma warmed his nostrils, but there was none of the soul lift a musician might come to rely on. Instrument and inner being never met. As he played, the excruciating minutes wore on, and he grew all the more resentful of the outsiders who hovered on the edge of the Center's torchlight, consulting with the Wise.

Just moments in the village! The outsiders were already souring the Sundown proceedings and had presumed to approach the Wise without a booger of ceremony. The old stranger, the gray-head, moved about assuredly, and seemed to have enough education to make himself understood to the Wise. He was speaking in a makeshift communication bolstered by silly hand signs. The young one followed him closely, like a singed kitten.

Both of the outsiders wore those clingy machine-skins, the kind that had never wrapped an animal. Their faces and hands were milky white and showed not one colored honor marking, no mumble scars, not even an appreciable sun scorch. As he saw them now, he knew them to be exactly what the Wise had historically called these wayfarers from the cities, stragglers from the clusters of human decay: the Fungus People. Yes. Soft and deathly white scavengers.

When the music stopped, every set of Pa bones was in place in the rack as if they had never been played. Tension hung in the air thicker than pyre smoke. The crowd was quiet with anticipation, a collective breath held. Tha'Enton pushed away from the quarter sphere and strode into the crowd, the only sound being the clatter-clack of his shin guards.

Laddo the barterer stopped him on the Center's causeway and threw a long laugh into Tha'Enton's face—a mild insult, an uninventive one. But the barterer grew sober when he felt the stinging splash of Tha'Enton's urine against his thigh—a serious insult, a deadly one. Laddo about-faced and, elbowing a path through the bemused and raggedy gawkers, scurried back to his display table mounded with refuse of questionable value. There, he consoled himself by smacking and lashing his naked little helpers.

When Tha'Enton reached the Wise he saw that he was expected. The Wise, after all, anticipated everything. To the outsiders, Tha'Enton knew, the Wise was perceived as three bodies, three men. But it was not so. The Wise thought and reasoned as one in impeccable logic. Mentally, they were one and inseparable. Oh, there were awkward times that they had to be considered as individuals for day-to-day living, and only then could they be called by bodily designations.

"Tha'Enton, Sounder and Defender, you will go with these Fungus People and collude in their endeavor. They come to us at the will of the son of Rutherford Cross himself. While you will protect them and give them aid, you also will see that these matters of the Fungus People—this festering—will be confined to the cities and never spread to civilization."

Tha'Enton saw that the unschooled gray-head had turned to one of the Wise, the Father, thinking the words had come from his lips alone.

The musician's chest grew several inches and his braids of brown hair fell away from it. "Wise, perhaps the festering is with us now and should be cast into the pyres," he said.

"No!" scolded the Wise. "If there is any good among the Fungus People, it lies with this man, the old one, and those who follow. He lives not in the dung-heap cities, but under a mountain far east. Go and help."

"And when I have destroyed this festering that the outsiders speak of?"

There was a quiet moment in which it was decided that the gray-head had not understood the last exchange. The Wise reasoned, "When the festering is scorched away, you may commemorate the day with a new musical composition biddled from the bok of these two men's skulls."

The younger of the two outsiders was feeling braver now,

even smiling, and he extended his right hand in the friend-ship gesture of the Fungus People. Tha'Enton smiled too, baring his sharpened yellow teeth and urinating on the young man's palm.

21
A Wet Book

". . . Well, ya can say I bugger everything I touch, ya. How many years would ya say Moberly had been building her inn? Fifteen 'er twenty, I gully—house and barn, brewing setup, all the additions." He wiped his nose on his forearm, scratched at his beard, and stared back at the campfire. "So now there's Security men pawing through her place. If they don' find me, they'll be pig-pissed. And then they'll find *something*.

"They're lookin' for me now. You 'er right, Pec-Pec. No . . . there's no goin' back. I'll be buggered, probably, any city I go to. Ya shoulda let me take my truck, least. *Their* truck. Now I got nothing. I'm in the wastelands alone with a crazy pokin' magician, and I got nothing. Just some maps and a few centimes. *No travel papers,* boogie. No equipment. That's all in the *truck*. But no, says the crazy poker. I canna go back to the truck. Go back to the truck, he says, and I die. Huh."

Anton Takk saw there would be no response, and he continued the monologue to fill the condemning quiet. "No.

None of that Supply housing for me anymore. Not in Camp Blade, thank-you. Had my fill of that. . . .

"Hoo, I've a blabbery mouth—trouble for everyone. They took Nora, and I've told her about Ben Tiggle—his press and everything, that Cred Faiging Collapsible Press. . . .

"Do they keep 'em in the ground all the time? Nora Londi, I mean, at Blue Hole. They don't work down there all the time, do they?"

The fire sputtered on a sappy log.

"Ben Tiggle. Now there's one man, one good man I'd never hurt. He's my father, just about. Except for my *real* father, who's . . . Mmm."

Takk stared at his fingernails, and then at the dark-skinned man crouched near the fire, head bowed over an empty fish bowl. Beyond Pec-Pec, parked among the scrubby trees at the edge of firelight, was the magic man's truck, and Takk was struck by its appearance. Weeks ago in New Chicago, he seemed to remember, the truck had resembled a carnival wagon, some sort of gaudy gypsie ramshack. At the Moberly Inn, though, it had appeared at home among the Supply trucks. And now, maybe it was just the flickering of yellow light, the vehicle seemed . . . *rural*. Perhaps a milk wagon or a cattle cart.

Takk's mind turned to a tale Pec-Pec had told that day as they jostled across the prairie (a shocking badlands, by Norther standards). The story had concerned a magical animal—a fairy tale, really. A lizard the size of a man's finger, so it went, could crawl onto a leaf and turn just that shade of green. On a tree trunk, it would muddle to brown. It had the talent of disguising itself in just about any surroundings.

"Thrown into the air, then," Takk had asked, skeptical, "would the lizard turn clear like water and disappear?"

Hah. A fine question—it had rolled off the tongue so adroitly, spontaneously. The question, the absurd perplexity, hung there in the air unanswered like the hypothetical lizard itself. It was a prize question that Takk wanted to catch in his cupped hands and preserve—take it out whenever he desired, to look at it, think it over again.

Catch it in a bowl, in a blanket stretched out, on a sheet of paper.

Paper. Of course. Treasured, unanswerable questions could only be captured one way—on paper, written, and he forced himself up onto stiff knees and walked haltingly to the passenger door of the truck.

His canvas satchel, the last of his personal possessions, was on the seat. It contained an extra shirt, a pair of heavy socks, three bottles of ale. He pushed them all aside and found at the bottom the little pine case, six inches long, that he had crafted during idle hours in the Camp Blade warehouse. He flipped it open and drew out one of seven slender strips of soft metal—lead. He had traded on the black market for wheel weights salvaged from ancient trucks, and melted them down in a saucepan and then poured the glistening metal into a crevasse between floorboards in the warehouse, the straightest crack he could find. Once cooled, the fragile sticks of metal made suitable markers. He pulled writing paper from Pec-Pec's glove box—five-by-seven-inch sheets pressed between two thin boards and wrapped around by twine.

Takk returned to the light of the fire and bent his tired legs again to lower himself onto a stone perch. He unbound the paper and slapped a sheet onto the wood cover, knowing its hard surface would make the dull markings most legible.

Now, how did he remember it? "Thrown into the air," he had asked, "would the lizard turn clear like the air and disappear?" Yes. He began scribbling. Pec-Pec had been driving and he had snorted his admonishment as they bumped across the prairie—"You crazy"—but his eyebrows had risen and the magic man had grown silent for hours as he seemed to take the proposition seriously—shaking his head, whispering to himself.

Crazy. Takk knew crazy. Outposts like Camp Blade were famous as homes of the befuddled and the berserk.

Pec-Pec was crazy: a braided wild man who had coddled a peculiar fish in his hands this evening, *swallowed it,* and had passed out perilously close to the campfire. Takk looked up from his writing. Pec-Pec had not moved for twenty minutes. Could the magic man, as he called himself, have choked on his slithery pet?

Takk decided to try to wake him.

When Pec-Pec saw the moving headlights from afar, he grew intensely attracted to them, a mothlike instinct. Disembodied, he flew through the blackness to the yellow discs and fluttered about them distractedly as rocks and rutted earth passed underneath.

The automobile was a new, government-issue jeep—fabric top, doors removed and stored in back. A man was at the wheel, a fellow with a hard-looking, angular face. Pec-Pec drifted to the man's left eye and slowly, in a liquid motion, enveloped the orb. When the man's eyelid blinked closed, and the eyeball rolled upward, Pec-Pec tumbled into the man's head.

There he found a book, a sopping wet volume which Pec-Pec opened. The pages were thin and flimsy, turning fluidly at the slightest touch. The first pages were white, and carried childhood images—a rotund mother, a sour-looking aunt, apple juice, a willow tree from which switches had to be cut by the little boy himself as he faced punishment. The center pages of the book grew pink, then bright red with vivid accounts of sexual encounters.

Doubt was an unfamiliar emotion to Pec-Pec, but here, perusing this private, scarlet parade of women, men, and animals, the magic man questioned his own methods. He paused. Never before had the dragon fish led him into such a sordid encounter. He thought of the ancient words *Curiouser and curiouser*.

His hands began flipping pages again.

The final several pages of the book were black, and Pec-Pec turned impatiently to the last few.

The first page among them showed a large man strapped to a table with heavy tape over his eyes. His jowly face rolled from side to side, and in astounding bursts of energy he lunged upward at his leather restraints, only to fall back again, tears gurgling in his throat.

Three Badgers, bearded and uniformed, chortled at the

effort. The Inspector, Mick Kerbaugh, was laughing too. He was unseen, of course, for these were his thoughts and memories.

At Kerbaugh's orders, a Badger quietly unbuckled Ben Tiggle's chest restraint. When Tiggle again bolted upward he flew from the table and crashed over the side, his feet still strapped in place and his head cracking against the plank flooring. More chuckles.

In that awkward position, Tiggle clawed at the tape over his eyes, groaning as it pulled away his eyelashes and eyebrows. In painful succession, hundreds of tiny volcanoes erupted on his face as each hair follicle burst. Finally the tape crackled down into a ring around his neck, and Tiggle squinted in the lamplight.

A Badger unstrapped his feet, and Tiggle's knees banged to the floor. Shakily, the large warehouseman stood and staggered toward a washbasin mirror. He rubbed his eyes and desperately examined his face in the glass. His brow and eyelids were inflamed, bloody, and virtually hairless, but there were none of cruel cuts and abnormal healing that Kerbaugh had promised. His eyelids had not been grafted together.

Tiggle felt no relief. He began to sob and felt excruciatingly weary. The information he had given . . .

The room rang with hearty guffaws.

The next black memory page reeked of foul smoke. The Moberly Inn was a roiling mountain of heat and flame, and the shutter on a ground-level basement window exploded into a shower of splinters as an ancient typewriter hurled through it.

In the basement, two sets of flailing arms clawed for a hold on the shattered window frame. One of the panicked men, Kerbaugh, howled into the blackness a vile harangue of expletives and orders. The meeker, yellow-haired bureaucrat acceded and frantically boosted the Inspector out of the window. Kerbaugh rolled onto the dirt, surrendering to a crippling coughing fit.

A steady tubular cloud of smoke now gushed from the basement window, occasionally obscuring the face of Gould

Papier, wide-eyed with terror. His bloody hands scrabbled over the frame of splinters and glass, looking for a grip.

Kerbaugh's hacking subsided. He sat up and glared down at his lap, soggy and black with soot and urine, and he pondered shamefully the paralysis that had crippled him in the basement—how Papier had desperately searched the machine room for an escape and finally coaxed him into helping toss the typewriter through the shutter.

Kerbaugh stood and spat. He staggered to the typewriter and lifted it by its front bar, slipping his hand under the mangled keys. He let the machine pendulum at the end of his right arm as he tested the weight, and then he heaved it back into the basement window from which it had come. When Gould Papier's face collapsed under the blow, the machine's carriage return bell rang a tiny *ping*.

The third memory page was one of ecstasy and lust. With the reverence of an art connoisseur, Kerbaugh followed the languid swinging motion of an object suspended from the barn rafter. He scratched at his crotch, and then hoisted his tunic away from his thighs, hoping to hurry the drying process.

The wavering firelight from the outside illuminated a row of seventeen oak ale vats spanning the far wall, as well as the bottle-capping machine with its pumplike handle and several dozen wood cases of capped quart bottles. All of it illegal. Kerbaugh drew a dusty bottle from one of the cases and groped about in the half-light until he found the opener—a simple metal fixture screwed to the workbench that supported the bottle capper. The opener bore a peculiar cursive inscription across its crest, *Coca-Cola*. Kerbaugh could not recall such a metal-working company.

He popped open the ale and tipped the bottle back, savoring its muddy sting. The soot washed from his throat, and he pulled again at the bottle, hard.

When he stopped with a loud sigh, the bottle was half empty. Kerbaugh, growing calmer, turned again to the figure swinging, creaking from the rafter. His chest broadened and eased at the dual sight of beauty and justice. It was that desk clerk, he knew, that Moberly woman. Three empty crates were scattered at her feet, kicked away just minutes ago. She had torched her own inn, hoping to incinerate the Inspectors who had discovered her press, and then hanged herself. A mercenary wretch, spiteful of the order and protection that Government stood for.

Kerbaugh crossed the dirt floor and reached high, grasping her knees. The swinging stopped. He opened his pocket knife, but the noose was impossibly out of reach. He considered stacking the ale crates again, but they looked rather flimsy, barely acceptable support even for a suicide.

"Pig fuck."

Kerbaugh glanced about on the off chance that there might be a long-handled tool with a blade of some kind on the end. Pruning shears or something. No. He began to breathe heavily.

He mounted the crude stepladder to the loft, and at the top found a rickety flooring covered with pigeon droppings. The loft had not been used for decades, the Inspector observed, and he edged carefully to the rafter from which Moberly had hanged herself.

Walking the rafter erect was out of the question—there was nothing to hold for support. So Kerbaugh nervously eased himself into a sitting position on the beam and, with one hand in back and the other in front, he pushed himself daintily along the support, trying not to pick up any more splinters than necessary. He coughed, and breathed even more rapidly.

Slicing through the rope was quick work, with the help of the tension from Moberly's weight. When her body slammed to the floor, he grinned uncontrollably. It had been such a massively satisfying day: a fortress afire, a villain vanquished, and now he could have his way with her. He snapped his knife closed, replaced it in his tunic pocket, rolled over to hang from the rafter, and dropped to the floor.

Pec-Pec paused at the last page, the image of the hanging woman, and tore the page out of the binding. It came away easily. He ripped out another black page with a furious flourish, then another, then dozens more, several at a time, and wadded them into his right hand. When he reached the blood-red pages he yanked them out, too.

The magic man began to tear seven pages at once from the soggy book—the last three pink pages and four white ones—when there came a ghostly, excruciating blow to his right jaw. Pec-Pec's vision blurred into a swirling cluster of stars, and then the stars gradually dwindled to just a few, which were set into a black background. He was gazing at the night sky as Anton Takk slapped his face.

"Hey, Pec-Pec," Takk said, "you fainted."

Pec-Pec felt as if he had fallen from a building onto concrete. Wincing, he forced himself up onto an elbow, scrambled for the empty glass bowl and belched the dragon fish into it.

As he lay back again, his gold-tipped braids flopping into the dirt, Pec-Pec whispered, "Takk, you pig's ripe asshole, you almost killed me."

"I was worried that—"

"I will tell you again: When I enter the trance, do not touch or speak to me. As things are now, my business is not finished, and I do not believe that I can return to where I have just been."

"So I have done more damage, no?" Takk said meekly.

Pec-Pec's eyes glowed a dull red. "Actually," he replied, "you might have saved a man's life. And stopped me from a murder."

Ben Tiggle had taught his young charge Anton the constellations—a bawdy version of them anyway—and it was on this sleepless evening that Takk was admiring from his bedroll the star formation described to him as a large drunken woman crawling home from a tavern. She was named Ursala Major.

Takk imagined that she was humming to herself as she struggled up the boardwalk, an aimless droning that one would scarcely want to call a tune. And then in a sobering flash Takk realized that he really was hearing that sound. A car engine, obviously, not a humming drunk.

He wanted to stand up and . . . and what? Logic intervened. The car was far off, and it was much preferable not to disturb his blankets and lose the accumulated warmth. Whoever the motorist was, he would surely miss their off-road campsite. But who would try to navigate these crumbling highways in the darkness? Takk drew his arms up against his chest and returned his attention to Ursala Major.

22
Hannibal

"That goddamned Rafer *pissed on my hand!* And now he's part of our team? A team to do what, no one seems to know."

"I want you to trust me on something: I have crisscrossed this territory two dozen times—"

"This is the Wise Ol' Man speech coming."

"—and the world works, or at least blunders about randomly, in ways I had never imagined—okay, I'll say it— *when I was your age*. You may roll your eyes now. But we need Tha'Enton for our mission, I know that, though we may think of him as a barbarian."

"We may need him, if he doesn't chop our throats and drink our blood first."

"When he boogies out like you've seen, well, he goes off into the woods like that at night to protect us. Those are his orders—he is titled a Defender of his people, and by Rafer law he must protect us as well—we're important allies."

"You have a few grunts and mumbles with those three

half-dead pig pokers, and you come up with an awful detailed notion of their intentions.''

The older man sighed. ''I have dealt with the Rafers for decades, know the language almost. I know these things by now, plumb. And those 'half-dead pig pokers' have not aged by one gray whisker since I first met them—the same three Rafers. They know something we don't about time, aging, collective thought, I don't know what else.''

''Oh, probably cannibalism, funeral pyres, nudity, tooth-sharpening—lots of things we could learn.''

Webb sank into thought and ran an index finger across his bristly chin. ''Um, I promised to tell you about Hannibal,'' he said finally.

''The town where we crossed the big river, the Oh-one-one.''

''Well, a man. A man born there, and also called Hannibal, maybe it was a nickname. In the old times, he needed a way to cross these mountains we're coming to, the Rocky Mountains. He was a revolutionary, like us. He had an army and weapons and to win the war he had to get them across the Rocky Mountains.''

''To the Big Ocean?''

''Nah, farther. Farther to this huge porker of a city, Los Atlantis, well beyond the mountains. It finally sank and created the Big Ocean. But to get there, to cross this terrain, Hannibal had to find some unknown, unthought-of transportation.''

''He invented jeeps!''

''There were no automobiles at all then. They had not even conceived yet of the machines that would fight the Big War. The answer was elephants.''

''What?''

''Elephants. Huge plumb suckers, these animals. They used to roam these grasslands, and the Rafers back then would hunt them. They were like pigs, hunnerd times larger, if ya can gully that. With long windy noses to grab with.''

''Umm. Sometimes I think I'm just not as religious as you are.''

''Well, no. We're speakin' history, not religion. But you're missing the point. Thing is, out of our home, away from the Blue Ridge, people, animals, the whole world is different. If we want to survive, we learn to work with the new worlds we find. Hannibal found the elephant herds and used them to carry him and his men across the Rockies. Out there"—he pointed—"the Rocky Mountains."

Gregory did not reply for a moment, and then remembered a conversation he had heard inside a fortified compound far back east, weeks ago. "Your point, then, is something like what Mr. Faiging was saying about Pec-Pec?" he asked.

"Yes. The Rafers just look at the world differently. . . ."

"Back'ards."

"From most. To them, civilization—goodness, art, security, the whole plumby thing worth living for—is spread across the wilderness. Cities are disease."

"Pec-Pec thinks like that? We're hauling into scrubland to find a man, some poking magic man thief who thinks like that? Like a Rafer?"

"Um. He not only thinks like that, but he *is* a Rafer, technically. I gully he's something like the *king* of Rafers. Not that he ever lived among them—no. Visits now and then, fades in and out. They think of him as an itinerant god, always on the fringes where he can never be seen fully, never grasped as a whole." Rosenthal Webb laughed. "The more I tell about Pec-Pec the more he sounds a bollocks. But believe, Pec-Pec would not have sent us to find Tha'Enton just to get our throats dillied. Any bugger who's spent a lifetime eluding the Monitor can't be all bad, eh?"

"You mean, the Monitor's tracking this Pec-Pec, an' *we're* going to meet up with the man? Oh, poke—"

"No. I meant *totally* eluding the Monitor. My word is that—up to now, anyway—the Government doesn't even know he exists."

"But ho up a minute! You said you hadn't seen Pec-Pec in a year. And when you asked Cred Faiging about him, you were barely trustful. How is it now that *Pec-Pec* sent us to pick up this bone-rattler?"

Rosenthal Webb had to stop and think, staring up from his sleeping bag into the nighttime star blanket. The memory was there in his mind clear as the moon: The dark-skinned magic man with his knotty little mustache telling him to

visit the Wise and ask them about the warrior who also is
a musician. But no, he *hadn't* met with Pec-Pec since a
year ago, long before this mission had been set in motion.
So why was he so damned sure he and the magic man had
recently had a conversation?

Webb propped himself up on his elbows and stared into
the red coals of the camp fire long into the night.

23
Flying Machines

Nora Londi followed the monster through the blackness of the rocky tunnel until it widened into a massive, dimly lit cavern. Her first impression was that she was overlooking a city at night. Below there were orderly legions of yellow and red lights in precise patterns. Neighborhoods and thoroughfares more expansive, even, than New Chicago's.

As her eyes grew accustomed to the illumination, she saw that the lights were not so distant. This was a cavern the size of twenty tobacco barns, and its floor was filled with rows of blocky cabinets, machines dotted with innumerable bulbs and gauges, some of the little lights winking on and off as their functions were called into play.

The dreadful beast stood in the center of the "city," near a horseshoe-shaped desk laden with control panels and keyboards—an assemblage that gave Londi a sickening apprehension. The large bull-faced man was waving her on, beckoning and mumbling unintelligibly under the whir of machinery. His muscular mounds of skin glistened in the odd light—perhaps a little greasy from too many cannibalistic meals, Londi told herself. She descended the stony slope until she hit the polished stone flooring and looked back: The llama Diego and little Loo had emerged from the black tunnel and were following.

". . . and stand right here in the center of the universe," the hunched man was saying when she came within hearing range. "I don't expect you to understand all of this, Nora. But these are thinking machines. They collect information, store it, assimilate and analyze. The way . . . just the way a brain does."

"You thought there was a real Government? Well, not in New Chicago, no." There was a wet hiss as he breathed deeply. He motioned grandly around the dark room. "There is a town of note takers and taxers, builders, Badgers, Inspectors. Bureaucracy. Mmm, to carry out my orders, but most of those groundlings have no idea I really exist. Or, at least, where I exist and in what form."

"From here, one man—with assistance from little Loo—can control every population center on the continent. We monitor, regulate, all use of teletype, telephone, wireless. You won't believe this, because you can't see them, but there are actually ancient flying machines high above us. So high up that there is no air there. *My* flying machines. I found 'em, figured them to be. One even has an meanly powerful camera. There is not much my machines don't see or hear."

Londi leaned against the rounded desk, feigning nonchalance. She poked at the nearest keyboard. It was made of worn plastic and carried the sheen of a well-used knife handle.

"These thinking machines," Londi said, "that's Old Age talk. They had the thinker boxes and the flying machines. There's none of that now."

The big man laughed. "There's none of that, maybe, except mine! The computers have been here for centuries, perfectly preserved in the cool and dry of these caves. I had to build the turbine to power them. Then took another ten years to gully the machines themselves."

Diego clopped up beside Londi and sniffed at the keyboard. Loo pulled him away by his neck.

Irritated, Diego asked, "Fly, hooma, machine? No . . . ooom, not legal."

The monster's bovine face brightened with pride. "I *made* that illegal!"

"So you would have the only ones?" asked Londi.

"Oh, don't say it so sour. We must have some *control!* Technology, the reading and the writing." He shuddered. "These things are for me. For the Government. That way the Government embodies all good, all progress. It cannot fail.

"But those flying machines, not even I actually have one to ride in, as the ancients used to. Mine are all in the sky. To bring them down would destroy them."

Diego murmured pensively, "Hoooorma."

"And what's this little stick woman got to do with running the Government?" Londi asked gesturing at Loo.

"She talks to the computers so well that it saves me weeks of time, weeks of typing out the thinker box talk. It all has to do with that language she developed once she, uh, misplaced her tongue." The man smiled, his thick lips twisting grotesquely, and pulled the cover off of a microphone on the counter. "She speaks into this instrument with that ooonga-oooonga talk—you've heard how she speaks? It's a language based on tone levels and changes in pitch. Think of it as a language that climbs up and down stairways, while ours remains on the ground. Vertical, as opposed to horizontal."

Londi stared blankly, but he continued, "Loo's language is much more suited to binary logic, which is how these machines think. When I command the thinker boxes, the computers, it takes me twenty times the effort."

Londi shook her head, understanding little of the explanation. "I suppose there's a reason you've shown us?"

"Oh, you killed one of my Transport men, and while doing that blundered into the center of Government. You are bright and strong, and you are either an asset to me or a danger. Mmm, now. You owe me a body." He scratched at his belly. "You will either work with me and, humph, join the gene pool, or you will die. Either way, you will never leave our community. You see that, don't you? That you owe me a body—one way or another?"

"Not much of a choice."

"Then in the spirit of cooperation, you will tell me about your friends."

"I don't have any friends."

"The friends you spoke of earlier. Knights, you called them, using chess terminology. Yes, I was aware of them. But they can't know you are here, can they? They must think you are at Blue Hole. They will be captured there—easily. It's not only my largest prison camp, but also a training ground for Security. I like to have them refine their, uh, interviewing techniques on the prisoners."

Londi was at a loss. She had mentioned companions as a bluff, and now she was told that someone actually seemed to be on the follow. But then she had a wry thought: There *was* one bastard's name she didn't mind giving.

"It's probably Anton Takk."

Loo groaned, disappointed. Londi turned and saw that the little woman had her razorlike flier's knife in hand.

"She's buggered," said the large man. "We already knew the answer. And if you lied, I had promised Loo she could have a little nick of your tongue. Let's hope you continue to cooperate. Or you might have to learn Loo's language.

"You see, we take visitors from the outside quite seriously. No one must know where we are. If the location of this canyon became known all across Merqua, we would have to move immediately. And I hate moving—every forty or fifty years is often enough." He sighed. "And now I've got the thinker boxes—a whole cavern full of thinker boxes, which would not be a simple thing to transport surreptitiously."

The Monitor's jaw muscles bulged nervously. "If I had to move now because of your friends, I would get quite upset," he said sternly.

Londi felt queasy, and as her vision began to blur, she heard Diego's hoofs clatter nervously. She put a hand on the desk for support. Anton Takk. That Northland rube—out here? Oh, bugger. "Yeah I'll, uh, cooperate. Course I will."

"Yes," he responded, suddenly cheerful. "And now shall we entertain ourselves with a real game of chess? Did you know that even the ancients considered it an ancient game—it's that old? They say that there are two things that not even the firebombs can eradicate: Mankind and chess. We *do* like to keep killing each other, don't we?"

24
Driving

" . . . And then Pec-Pec, the son of god Rutherford Cross, came among us weeping. He gave us knowledge where we had little, he gave us children where few could be born, he gave the unending life to those who would be Three As One, The Wise. And as he gave these gifts he then took away as well. He forbade that ever the children of Rutherford Cross should use the tools by which explosion may tear at flesh . . . "
　—From the writings of Ligkh Priest Lit Mannah, 2UH3.

"The dragon fish *seems* to be confined to his bowl. Words *seem* trapped in a closed book. Love *seems* to dangle between your legs." He rethought the last point and grimaced. "Well, none of these things are captive."

There was no response.

"I will try to explain it again. In another way. Look at my hands—I am steering the truck just fine, around the boulders and craters. My feet hit the brakes at the right time.

We'd be dead if they didn't. So that is one state of existence. I am driving across the prairie.

"Yet I also am talking with you—I am trying to make you understand that we will not go to Blue Hole. Scream, scream, scream, go ahead, boogie. We must go to a canyon south of there. That is a second state of existence. I communicate with you, and that has nothing to do with bouncing across these hills. I can do both of these things at once. It is as if I have two minds, or I am in two places at once— or, if I were a much stronger person, that I actually were in all places at all times.

"But I am not this powerful person. If the driving here gets very difficult, if there is rain and I cannot see well, or if . . . Oh! Sorry! . . . if there are many more craters like *that* one, then I must give more of myself to the driving and less of myself to our conversation.

"And so it is somewhat in the same way that while I sit beside our camp fire I can also be, uh, sharing ideas with a man who is many miles away. To reach that man, to enter his mind, takes very hard work. So while I am also sitting beside the fire, I cannot do so much—it is best to close the eyes and not move. This makes me dangerously hurtable, as you found out, but these are the risks.

"It was hard work, meeting with this man—*entering his mind*. You talk about how badly you feel about what happens to people you meet, particularly people you love. Well, this man—this man whose mind I entered—I have not love for him at all. He does harm to many people, and had terrible things planned for you. Still, I do not think that he deserved what I fear I have done to him.

"We must live by certain good ways or—who knows?— we could destroy civilization. The way . . . the way an angry child tears apart a book. Anton, there are things we cannot even wish on our own. . . . Anton, are you listening? Are you awake?"

That afternoon Anton Takk dreamt that he could fly.

25
The Walking Dead

Tha'Enton was beginning to think he had exhausted the musical possibilities of riding on top of a metal beast, the van. His music here started, as always, with sounds provided by the environment—the constant whine of the engine and the whooring of wind in his flared nostrils. There was the less rhythmic crunch and scratch of tires against gravel and the clattering jeep following behind, and to this he added his own mallets pounding against the van top (his *practice* mallets—not the fine performance pieces he used on the ban-ott drums).

As the van angled northwest across the Redlands, Tha'Enton had grown fond of sitting cross-legged, facing forward, near the front of the van. Musically, it was a strategic position: Within easy reach were the low tones of the center of the roof behind him, the tight and tinny throppings afforded by the edge where the metal skin wrapped over the roof supports, and the tick-tick of the windshield.

He bokked the windshield only sparingly, but with great relish, for the surprise of it seemed to drive the gray-head at the wheel gullybonkers.

But for a musician used to the infinite permutations made possible by the Pa and its 718 pairs of bones, the van-top soundings had grown boring. Tha'Enton could easily fall into spells of silence as he scanned the scorched badlands, mentally hunting jack deer, those antlered, sheep-sized rabbits crouching in the scrub. He would spot one of the cowering creatures, gauge the van speed and distance, then imagine flinging a tosser disk.

It was during such a meditation that they topped a hill in the red desert and the roadblock, such as it was, came into view. A government jeep had been pulled across the highway and a lone figure stood at its side. Curiously, any vehicle could have detoured the obstruction by a mile on either side—if the driver were willing to risk the caugi cacti puncturing the tires.

Tha'Enton leaped to a crouch on the balls of his feet, and in the same motion he slipped the Sounder sticks into the quiver on his back and drew out a twenty-inch blade. In the left hand, as a precaution, he cupped a tosser disk with its dozen deadly spines. The Defender back-paced to the rear of the van roof, never taking his eyes off of the man in the road. He tapped the metal roof, hoping the gray-head would pull over before coming too close to the roadblock. When there was no response—the gray-head probably thought he was making more music—Tha'Enton uttered a mild Rafer curse and flipped backward onto the gravel, hoping that young idiot Fungus Man following in his jeep would not run over him.

The risk had to be taken: A Defender cruising into danger atop a vehicle like a hood ornament was no Defender at all. When he hit the gravel, he immediately frog-leaped into the air again, using the compression against his leg muscles for added spring. The timing was almost right. The young Fungus Man's jeep passed just under him, and Tha'Enton's heels scraped the canvas top. He landed awkwardly and hard, but pleased at having avoided a thorough trouncing by the knobby wheels.

As the Fungus People pulled their vehicles to a stop, he cautiously edged to the right, making sure the autos blocked sight of his approach. He leaned forward into a salamander run—his body at a low incline of about thirty degrees to the ground. The momentum and an occasional knock on the ground with his left hand kept him from falling face first into the red sand. His waist-skin parted around the legs and flared silently behind. It was a Hunter's run, more intended for dashing low and unseen through wooded underbrush, but it was also serviceable among the rocks and wash gulleys of the Redlands.

Tha'Enton sailed down the road bank, zigzagging in the lowland until he had passed all of the vehicles. The fool gray-head was approaching the stranger in the road, while the younger Fungus Man was looking back down the highway, apparently thinking he would find an injured Rafer writhing in the gravel. Come to think of it, Tha'Enton told himself, his right ankle was starting to burn and stiffen up a bit.

He mounted the roadbed again, still at full tilt, and ran back soundlessly across the gravel until he stopped at the stranger's tailgate. He would search the stranger's auto first, and perhaps have some clue about what the man intended. There were six large fuel cans, and five of them rang full when Tha'Enton knuckled them softly. There were flashlights, a rolled tent, cartons of food. Much of the personal belongings, apparently, were in the three canvas saddlebags—which meant that the stranger intended to use pack animals, probably into a remote part of the mountains.

But when he unsnapped the first of the saddlebags, his heart tightened into a fist of fear and hate. He pulled out a grotesque hunk of black metal that he recognized as a pistol—and only a Government man of the Fungus People would own such a thing. He had to take the unholy object, for it was a powerful weapon that had killed many Defenders. He would find a way to destroy it. The gun was an awkward fit for his quiver, but he jammed it in anyway, creating a vile imbalance on his back.

The three Fungus People were staring strangely at each other when Tha'Enton crept up behind the Government man, blade ready, feeling confident that no other weapons were in sight. There was only one thing to be done with a Government man, and Tha'Enton noted with amusement that this one had a particularly large and oddly shaped skull. What sound would it make, once hollowed and dried?

The gray-head's jaw dropped at the sight of the Defender, and the old Fungus Man stepped around the stranger with his hands up. With his stuttery knowledge of the civilized tongue, the gray-head managed to say: "No kill yet. This Fungus Man harmless."

The Defender snarled and spat at the old man's foot. The spittle raised a poof of red dust near his boot, but the gray-head would not back off. It would be easy work to end this foolish mission now, Tha'Enton told himself. He envisioned lopping through the gray-head's wrists, a disk-toss at the young one's throat, and perhaps a whirl-kick to snap the Government stranger's spine. But that was against the instructions of the Wise, and if they entered Tha'Enton's mind and found the truth he could end up on a pyre, alive maybe. He sheathed the blade, which scraped sickeningly against the pistol in his quiver.

He pulled at the stranger's shoulder and the man turned cooperatively. It was another of the Fungus People with the peculiar habit of scraping the hair from his face—often the sign of a Southlander or a city man—although this one had not done so for days. His tunic was of flimsy machine-skin, and Tha'Enton wrinkled his nose at its filthy odor.

The stranger's eyes were unfocused, the sockets cavelike, and his right iris was split vertically like a feline's. A string of phlegm dangled from a nostril. His shoulders drooped and his hands hung limply to his thighs. It was a shocking sight, for he had seen the same posture, the same vacant face, the cat's eye, only on the handful of Walking Dead among his own village—and only the Wise, or a powerful Ligkh Priest, could do such a thing to a man.

He remembered from early schooling the words of the ancient god Rutherford Cross: "The Walking Dead are child spirits I have set free. Once men, they are now my children, forever. Do them no harm."

Instinctively, Tha'Enton studied the landscape to the far horizon in all directions. It seemed empty, but the Defender was not so sure. And his right foot was beginning to swell.

26
Song for the Ramshack Man

The indignities and absurdities were mounting. Gregory had been staring at his knuckles over a steering wheel for two months now, and they were turning a grotesque white and red from chapping and incidental nicks and scratches. They had adopted as compatriots on this dubious mission a foul-smelling primitive preoccupied with weaponry and rhythms and an unaccountably mindless New Chicagoan—harnessed now in Gregory's passenger seat—who was equally mal-odorous for his lack of bladder control.

And Rosenthal Webb, the legendary revolutionary in charge of this sad menagerie, was obviously operating with one wheel in the sand. Not only was he inclined to obtain fuel, auto parts, or entire engines through despicable means, but he seemed to have more confidence in the grunts and howls of that Rafer drum-beater than his own assistant. It was rare that Gregory found Webb navigating scientifically, by standard compass-and-map calculations. Maps of this region may not be the most reliable, but they have, sup-posedly, some foundation in logic. But the old man—the old man seemed to make his directional decisions now based on the nonsensical blitherings of their two new companions, one a murderous witch doctor or something, the other literally an idiot. Because of the New Chicagoan's mental state, Gregory had come to think of this as "dead reckoning." It was a joke he kept to himself.

They were pushing farther and farther past the edge of carefully charted territory without a clear destination in mind. There could be no more fuel depots out here, even those with perilously rusting tanks and hand pumps. For food now they had only dried goods and any of the odd beasts they dared kill and eat. In the middle of the glowing Redlands, they had arrowed a large rabbit-looking creature with antlers. Tha'Enton and Webb devoured it, while Gregory had an extra ration of jerky.

The entire mission was going contrary to orders, and surely they all faced censure when they reported back to the Committee—if they returned alive at all. They were ordered to find Anton Takk and help him hide ("Ya, ya, soon," Webb kept saying.) Before even leaving the eastern mountains, Webb had stocked up on hand bombs and blades and all manner of destructive gear forbidden by the Committee—a Committee intent on an age of peace.

Hah. Webb was a lunatic.

The Redlands had abruptly given way to this range of Rocky Mountains, a ruined and simmering prairie void of people and rising suddenly into awesome walls of rock. Early this morning Webb had insisted that they leave the main road, which was crumbling but perfectly navigable. Gregory had the jeep today. And now, to Gregory's amusement, Webb's van up ahead was scrabbling awkwardly up the fading trail that wound among the firs and aspens. Although the van's huge fuel tank was now less than half full, its sloshing back and forth presented further stability problems.

Branches battered the sides of their autos, and Gregory speculated morbidly that it would not be long before the van overstepped its gravitational limitations and crashed onto its side, perhaps sliding down the mountain. Gregory smirked at the sight of the Rafer clinging desperately to the van's roof. As a native of the eastern mountains, Gregory enjoyed the sight of a flatlander panicking in the hill country.

He plowed a sweaty hand through his blond locks and glanced at the man strapped into the jeep seat beside him, hoping that the Inspector, as Webb called him, would not have to urinate again soon. Even when Gregory anticipated the need, it was a messy and demeaning chore. And bouncing along this rocky terrain, he knew, could torture a bladder.

The Inspector was awake now, and he watched the trail ahead like an eager child, leaning forward and tugging at the straps holding him in the seat. He seemed to be mumbling a nursery rhyme, and Gregory hoped that he would not break out into another full-voiced, incomprehensible song, as he was wont to do.

These were cruel mountains, Gregory told himself, so much more threatening than the gentle slopes of the Blue Ridge in his home district. He thought of the hillside bunkers in which he had grown up, and he sighed—it was an odd upbringing, he knew, but the remote revolutionary compound was home, and he longed for the comfort of those earthy chambers of cool and dark.

Webb's van stopped abruptly, and the barbarian back-flipped off its top and melted into the underbrush. Gregory stopped, too, set the parking brake, and only then noticed the sorry little ramshack tucked amid the boulders and aspens. It was an unreliable structure, Gregory noted, and in the next breeze it could easily become a lean-to shouldering the mountainside, or just a pile of rotted timbers and shingles.

Beyond the cabin was an equally dilapidated truck, its sides decorated with thick rooster tails of mud and its bed dubiously sheltered by plank-and-post framing. There were several llamas wandering about freely, munching scattered hay. They had presented the new arrivals with a frieze of lackadaisical stares, and already appeared bored again.

Webb appeared at Gregory's jeep door and opened it. He looked immensely pleased with himself and said, ''We take pack animals from here—llamas, they're the best in these parts. This is the way the Inspector had mapped out, apparently, before he . . . well, before his brain cracked a cylinder. His presence might help us some right now.''

Gregory asked himself sardonically just how many among them had ''cracked cylinders.'' He squinted at the low sun and hoped that they would sleep here before turning the mission over to a train of glorified goats.

A wide board functioning as a door clattered away from the little cabin, and a wiry man emerged cautiously, glancing about and finally striding toward Webb and Gregory. He was garbed in a loose arrangement of stitched skins, and his flesh was a barky gray-brown.

Webb cupped his hands around his mouth: ''We're here to buy llamas. We're ganging on—deep in.'' Webb jabbed a thumb westward.

The mountain man spat, pressed his nostrils together, and released them again. ''I got no llamas.''

Gregory frowned and swept his hand across the landscape. ''You've got''—he paused to count—''seven, eight.''

''No llamas for sale. Maybe now you carry your trucks. Yeh-heh. Carry your trucks yourselves so deep into the bumpers. They carried *you* this far.''

Webb interjected. ''We've got any kind of trade, by plumb. Government chits that'll pass anywhere. . . .'' This drew a blank stare from the mountain man. ''We have Rafer bronze disks,'' Webb continued, ''gasoline, good steel tools—we might even give up one of the trucks. Not just for a few animals, but we could work something out.''

The shack dweller was unswayed. He stepped up to Gregory and thumped the young man's chest and squeezed his biceps as if he were selecting market melons. ''You give me this boy,'' the mountain man said flatly, ''and you may have one llama.''

Gregory's jaw dropped, and he backed away. ''What!''

Webb laughed, and scratched his head. To his surprise he found a tick at the base of his neck. He yanked it free and studied it casually, not wanting to seem desperate in the negotiation. He mashed the tick between the tips of two fingernails.

''Gregory is not for sale,'' Webb replied. ''I had to hire him—temporarily. Humans, among us, are not for sale.''

The slender mountain man's face brightened. "Ha-ho!" he cried. "Now you understand! Llamas, among us, are not for sale. You will all come inside and we will discuss how to go about hiring llamas—temporarily. And you must meet my partner. We have been waiting days for you."

Webb's and Gregory's eyes met. At that moment a chatter of woody rhythms wafted through the aspens, and the mountain man glanced up into the dimming sky as if to find the source. "And you have the forethought to bring a good bonesman with you," the mountain man told his guests. "Listen to that! Very cultured of you. Do you know what his song says? He is talking to me, but modesty prohibits a full translation. He says, 'Hello, god-man Pec-Pec.'" The dark man grinned. "He really is so excited that he is embarrassing himself. He says, 'You may sleep without fear as long as I am in the trees this evening.'"

Pec-Pec snorted. "I will teach him some humility. And perhaps he will teach me the bone-sounding."

27
Fireworks

Rosenthal Webb was twenty-three years old, clothed in rotting cotton and leaning against a brick wall. Before him on the sidewalk hummed the bankers and restaurateurs and bureaucrats of downtown New Chicago. At his right hand was a paper-wrapped bottle. He stared forward blankly at the scuffling of feet, a promenade made more frenetic by the prospect of the holiday parade: In forty minutes the papery dragons would dance by, followed by the Werewistles in their elaborately plumed costumes, then the Belbugs in their whirling pedal carts and silly tasseled berets, and finally the procession of open-back Transport trucks bearing New Chicago's Government elite in their holiday finery.

This stretch of Michigan Avenue was an easy shuffle and stagger from the sprawling bunkhouses the Government provided for the underprivileged. So it was not unusual to find the north wall of the Commerce Ministry lined with ragged men and women clutching their bottles.

But Rosenthal Webb was quite sober, as were his three compatriots mixed in with the crowd.

An elderly man who smelled like spoiled cheese crouched in front of Webb. He spoke through numbed lips: "My name's Big Tweed, an' I'd like to give *you* a bite of my sandwich." He produced from his pocket an object wrapped in oilcloth, but young Webb already was shaking his head vehemently.

Big Tweed looked hurt. He returned the sandwich to the pocket of his soiled sport coat and, in a surprisingly agile sweep of the arm, he snatched up the bottle at Webb's side. "I could stand the favor of a drink, though," he told Webb.

The young man's jaw dropped. "Give me that!"

Big Tweed upended the paper-wrapped container and sucked greedily. Webb lunged for it. The old bum gagged and spewed the clear liquid onto the sidewalk, causing two passing ladies to avert their eyes and quicken their pace. As the two men tussled, the bottle fell to the concrete with a dull thwack. Moisture darkened the wrapping.

Big Tweed issued a mournful "Aww." Webb listened in horror as his bottle began to hiss. The inner cannister had spilled and the chemicals were mixing.

Mentally, Webb began counting backward.

Five seconds . . .

He grabbed the bottle in his right hand and stood.

Four seconds . . .

Webb looked about the crowded street.

Three seconds . . .

He spied a large metal trash bin twenty feet away and began to sprint.

Two seconds . . .

As he slammed the bottle over the rim of the dumpster, it exploded—earlier than he had hoped—into an enormous column of flame that blackened the glass of the streetlight above. Passersby backed away, puzzled, wondering if the blast had been intended as some holiday amusement—fireworks, perhaps, gone awry?

Against the wall, three other ragged revolutionaries grabbed up their bottles and disappeared into the crowd.

Gasping for air, young Webb assessed the personal damage: hair and eyebrows singed away, right cheek scorched black and beginning to sting. Part of his shirt had been burned away at the center of his chest. And then he looked at his right hand.

28
Deep in the Bumpers

Please believe, I would not be scripting at this moment if
I could sleep. My ankle and knees joints are howling, and
I took a smack in the face during the march today that
leaves my top lip a split and swollen mess. A tooth is loose,
hinging in my mouth like a spring door.

I'm now halfway down my last bottle of Moberly's ale.
It tastes a gag of brush root, but it's deadening the pain.

Ho, the march. It wears on Pec-Pec not a whit. He bounds
across the mountainside ahead of us following a trail that
is apparent to none but him, then dances back—breathless
more from exhilaration than exertion—to tell us what's up
ahead for miles. The magic man is jubilant. His people are
gathered, he says, and the canyon we seek is less than a
week into the bumpers. There is a bullet to be found, he
says, an ancient bullet in the hands of the Government. Ho,
when he speaks of it I always lose the sense of him.

Tha'Enton is an odd buck from a south-center Rafer tribe.
I gully that Pec-Pec is a god to him, but most times he stays
distant with his guard duty. Last night, though, I witnessed
what I took to be a religious rite between the two. They

faced off, cross-legged. Pec-Pec spoon-fed to the warrior a small bowl of his bean soup, which none other of us will allow within nose's range. The talk between them was fast and raspy, like trees what rattle and snap in a windstorm.

We have a dozen beasts among us like I have never seen, llamas they are called. I imagine they are shrunken and furry horses what grew out of the radiation fields. What's most peculiar is that the llamas can speak—they make words, anyway, which I doubt they understand. Pec-Pec says the beasts to be quite intelligent, even though they gully not our language so well. They lean toward hornery, and tolerate humans only so far as need be for food and protection.

Six of the llamas are devoted solely to the hefting of hardware brought along by a sour old poker, name of Rosenthal Webb. He worries more over his cartons of hand bombs than he would a pregnant wife.

Webb says he's the one what sent money from the revolutionaries to Camp Blade. I had to fess the full story to him—how I really had made a bollocks of Nora Londi, and once I got the money I killed the Badger named Sgt. Krieger. The revenge I took was why I really had to flee, although Pec-Pec has given me hope of making right with Nora. Webb seemed pig-grin pleased to hear of the pounded Badger, and that was when he pounded my face. I found myself flat on my backpack, rolling among the rocks, with this gray-head rubbing his knuckles above me, saying, "That's for the lie, horse prick." And he hasn't spoken to me since.

Webb is a fright even to his assistant, a bucker name of Gregory. He told me before sacking out tonight that Webb had dillied with the facts some to get approval for his mission—that the official purpose was to hide me—but now it's clear Webb wants to ram a banger up the Monitor's canal.

If we must keep this up a week, then I am destined to be most miserable. At the rate I am losing possessions and taking a bashing, I will be nothing but a large naked bruise at the end of the trek.

—Anton Takk

29
The Bullet

Nora Londi did not trust this floor. It was neither wood nor stone. It was cracked and weathered, like an old man's skin, gapped in places and showing poured concrete underneath. If the Monitor were to be believed, it once glistened in one continuous sheen. But the Monitor had many a wild story in his ugly head.

She followed his galumphing white figure around the dim corridor until they came to an open hatchway. The Monitor pointed to the hatch door, which was open and shredded at the edges, resembling the lid torn from a sardine can.

"An ancient security cover," the Monitor grumbled, moisture gurgling in his throat. "It took me weeks just to get to the Bullet, but I knew I had to, if the old legends were true."

"Let's see this Bullet," Londi said, "and get on with it. I'd like to see the outside again. These walls feel so . . . close."

The Monitor ducked his head and forced his large frame through the hole. The red-haired logger followed and found herself standing on a circular catwalk. In the center of the catwalk, all right, was a Bullet—a very, very large Bullet. Metal. Painted white and blue and red. The size of a 200-year-old tree, pointed at the top, dozens of feet above. Below, where the Bullet widened slightly, were fins like the feathers of an arrow.

The tiniest boot-scrape on the catwalk produced ghostly echoes in the cylindrical room. The air smelled of decay, and some kind of foul burning that Londi associated with electricity.

"Here." The Monitor motioned with a wave of one pale hand and pointed down over the railing. "This is one of my early discoveries of which I was quite proud. You see the opening near the bottom—where a cable is running into the Bullet? Making that hookup was the result of months of frustrating deliberation."

"Oh, then congratulations."

"It is that hookup that allowed those thinker boxes you saw analyze the innards of the Bullet. I still have no idea why it won't fly."

" 'Cause it's illegal to fly. Oh yeah—and impossible."

The Monitor snorted.

"But I'm sure you could just bong over to New Chicago and pick up spare parts from a hardware store. Like I fixed a tractor once," Londi said.

The Monitor grumbled and leaned against the railing, resting on his muscley forearms. She saw dual reflections of herself in his sunglasses. "You don't take the Bullet seriously. I am showing you this so that you will under-stand—understand that you really are at the planet's center of power. Not just a communications center, not just a clearinghouse for wireless teletype messages, but actually the location of the world's most powerful weapon. Once I persuade it to fly, anyway. Remember, the fairy tales are true—*I am the Monitor.*"

"Impossible. This is ancient junk."

"No. You mention spare parts, and I think they might actually be available. You see this room?" The Monitor stamped on the metal catwalk and smiled at the booming echo. "There are a dozen of them just on this hillside—silos, they called them, like grain silos. Eleven of the silos opened, back during the Three-Hour War. You might call it Big Bang Day. Ten Bullets like this one actually flew. One other stayed in its silo and is now a pile of rust. And this twelfth silo never opened. This Bullet never flew. And never rusted.''

"Then this is a Bullet that misfired," Londi said. "If the ancients could not fire it, you could never hope to."

"It is possible," said the Monitor slowly, "that the ancients never intended to fire this one, that it was held back for strategic reasons. And that it is ready to fire even now.

"But if it does need repair, well, somewhere there has to be another Bullet. There were thousands just in the nearby sectors. When I know what I need, I will find the parts. It is just the final step in a long process."

"Some say that you was born on Big Bang Day," Londi said, narrowing her eyes. "But I'd give you, oh, forty or forty-five years' age."

"Specifically, four hundred thirty-five years," the Monitor said, smiling. "The combination of radiation and flesh produces no end of surprises, eh? What was deadly for all others was a source of longevity for me, it seems."

"But you haven't been in this canyon for . . ."

"Here? Oh, certainly not—I've been here a relative handful of years. You see, a man with a face like mine has to learn the art of behind-the-scenes manipulation—I couldn't govern publicly, could I?"

"Well, maybe—"

"No. Huh. Not possible. It's a lesson I learned early— my rearing was in an ad hoc orphanage, and a large and ugly rugger grows powerful in that environment if matters are handled in the right way. This was in a charred-out university. I set up shop in the library—scarcely left, had runners to break fingers for me.

"When I first came of age, I was a man of basements and back rooms, hired former longshoremen to do my bidding. If their tongues got too loose I would nick them out. That was early on down east, outside of Chautown, before the city-states were united."

Londi rubbed the bulb of her nose and squinted skeptically. "Umm, have we covered a hunnerd years of this yet?"

"Hah! Well, say, a hundred fifty years by then. Look, I have a small confession: I am a brilliant ruler in my own right, of course, but the fact is that I amassed an enormous amount of power simply by outliving all of the other politicians.

"But then came the electronic communication. It united the continent again and allowed me to operate even more remotely. I move often, you see, to stay ahead of those that would try to destroy me. But as long as I command the Government by wireless, what does it matter where I am physically?"

"So now you live in a hole in the mountains and you have one large Bullet," Londi observed. "Who will you shoot with your one Bullet? And what then?"

He coughed, spat over the rail, and then chortled, low. "We don't have the planet to ourselves. Yet. There are nearly five million people here in Merqua alone, a population growing all of the time. We have cities again where people speak of crowding as they haven't done for four hundred years—New Chicago, for instance, and Chautown.

"Overseas, past the Eastern Ocean—you hear the stories, don't you?—there are other, aggressive people, *their* numbers growing as well. Humans with their own ways, their own governments—and we know from ancient history what will happen once both governments have the means to travel freely from one land to another."

The Monitor fell silent for a moment, hoping the significance would sink in. "One well-placed Bullet at this time in history could set another civilization back centuries. We are blessed with this one large spear bequeathed to us by a glitch of ancient times. With its proper use, we can gain absolute superiority."

"You seem awfully eager to fire your Bullet," Londi said.

The Monitor coughed out a laugh. "It's those friends of yours, I suppose, that put me on edge—Anton Takk and his lot. Ya. I get wireless reports from Security, from innkeepers, from scavengers: Your fools have reached the mountains by now, and they've been moving in our direction, not northward to Blue Hole as I had first thought. They take bearing with such uncommon accuracy that I think it not coincidence.

"Oh, your friends will die easily," he added wearily. "But if they know the location of this canyon, then perhaps others do too. So yes, I'd like the Bullet to fly before I pull up stakes here. It'd be a pity to leave such a beautiful instrument still in the ground."

Londi peered up again, and imagined the stark blue sky that would be visible just beyond the silo cover.

"Before you take over the world, you'll have to figure out how to get the lid off this can," she said.

"It opens," the Monitor said.

"Oh? How?"

There was no answer.

Well, Londi told herself, then perhaps there's a way out of here.

30
No Report

The Monitor pondered the sparse readout on his computer terminal:

> *Code: A05–42 Brimley*
> *Destination: Monitor/Eyes only*
> *Routing: SATline II/Scramble*
> *Origin: New Chicago Central Wireless/Linex 3*
> *Message: Kerbaugh, Mick. Inspector.*
> *Status: No report.*

The Monitor tapped two keys, and the printer to his right burped out a permanent copy of the dispatch.

He pressed his right fist into his left hand, and four knuckles popped. Always the same. No report. Wearily he flipped off the terminal and removed his mirrored sunglasses, not needing the special lenses to read anymore. To human eyes, the room was now pitch black—but merely a soothing twilight to the Monitor. It was a small chamber, dominated by an oval down mattress.

Every few hours he checked by satellite relay to New

Chicago, and for weeks the message had not changed. First Nora Londi had stumbled into the hidden canyon; then Security, hoping to trap the conspirators of fugitive Anton Takk, tricked the warehouseman into fleeing cross-country from New Chicago; now, against regulation, Kerbaugh was not reporting in. Could Takk have doubled back somehow and killed him? He may have killed that Badger sergeant in a fit of fury—but was he capable of a calculated slay?

The Monitor grunted. Takk, once thought to be a dim-witted crate lifter, now appeared to be a crafty and lethal reprobate. How could Security not have known this? Maybe Kerbaugh had suffered the brunt of his own department's failing. Hmm. Yes.

There could not be a more meticulous and efficient Inspector than Kerbaugh. But even at his last report by wireless something was going wrong. The Monitor opened a folder and shuffled through a thin stack of computer print-outs to find it:

Code: A02–33 Kerbaugh
Destination: Monitor/Eyes only
Routing: SATline II/Scramble
Origin: Fallstown Inn wireless/Linex 44E94
Message: Takk covering tracks. Subject murdered inn
owner Moberly and Transportation escort Pa-
pier at last stop. Building and press burned
per procedure. In pursuit.

Murdered the inn owner? Really?

Takk. Papier. Kerbaugh. All were faceless names that the Monitor had manipulated from hundreds of miles away. Something like a chess match, no? There was power in that anonymity, and safety in distance. But these recent events would not do.

The Monitor pushed his chair back, rolled onto the bed, and studied the minute crystals in the ceiling rock. The thought of relocating his hidden headquarters made him tired. He had done it dozens of times, of course—forty years here, fifty there—and each time the logistics grew more complex. Exhausting. He must be mortal after all.

But if he must eventually abandon the canyon, what about his beautiful Bullet? It must fly soon. And perhaps it actually *was* ready to fly. Trajectory was programmed and guidance systems seemed operational. Warhead was intact, from what he could tell. Fuel was purified and reloaded. Engine and electronics all seemed fine in hands-on inspection.

All that he lacked was confirmation from the computer diagnostics programming left behind by the ancients. The Monitor had spent months reviewing the yellowed manuals line by line, rechecking the diagnostic linkups with the Bullet, and running the program again and again. The terminal screen would blink and flash with a rapid-fire array of component diagrams, a blizzard of algebraic nonsense, and then a sequence of geometric shapes. Finally the computer would blip up the single intelligible message to be gleaned from the program, one infuriatingly unspecific evaluation:

Abort launch.

Nothing more. Aaag. He made a mental note to pressure the salvagers to find new Bullets. If time allowed, perhaps he could substitute each part—gyro by gyro, circuit board by circuit board—until the diagnostics gave him the go-ahead to launch. That could take many months at best, perhaps more than a year. Hmm.

But what if the fault were with the diagnostics program itself? Perhaps the Bullet had really been in top form, even on Big Bang Day, but a reluctant computer had grounded it. A comma out of place. A typographical error buried in the muddle of base coding. A flub of the fingers recognizable only to a button pusher who died more than 400 years ago.

Perhaps the Monitor could just bypass the diagnostics and punch in the launch sequence—fire the bastard off. Was it that much of a risk?

Or perhaps he could find one more person to run through the entire assembly, top to bottom. One more mind capable of analyzing the most sophisticated piece of weaponry ever produced by the ancients. And *then* he would launch it.

Mmm. Cred Faiging, of course. He would never come willingly, so this assignment would have to be his last.

Could his services, his inventive genius, be sacrificed afterward?

The Monitor exhaled and decided to surrender to sleep.

Slowly he drew a hand down his moist snout, wondering if there would ever be a time, say in 200 years, that he could rule civilization face to face. And then he laughed: "Huh. Never."

If only he could produce offspring. It was an irony with which he had long ago made peace: long life, genius, and power—but a sterile body. How nice it would be to populate the world with little bull-faced immortals. He did his best, though, with breeding lesser beings, the soft and fragile humans. They would have to do.

As his breathing slowed and his eyelids drooped, he made another mental note: Find a fine mate for Nora Londi.

31
The Inspectors

Two armored trucks groaned over the hill, down past the lightning-damaged oak, and stopped mumbling at the gate to Cred Faiging's secluded compound. The driver of the first truck leaned onto his horn impatiently, blaring into the morning fog.

There was no motion in the entire five acres of rutted clay, trees, and buildings. Too early. The yard was encircled by a tall scramble of electrified steel-frame fencing and barbed wire, and was dotted with gray wood-frame structures, all one-story. Off to the left, set away from the fence, were the hulking garages, loading docks, and warehouses. To the right, farther down the hill, were the long, awkward-looking manufacturing huts with frosted side windows and solar boxes covering the roofs.

Straight ahead was the largest structure, the lab and living quarters, and just as the truck horn shrieked again, the front door sprang open. Kim, the inventor's skinny assistant, danced down the brace of steps as she ducked into the loop of her second bandolier. She shouted irritably in the direction of the trucks as she crossed the clearing—unintelligible from that distance, but no doubt an admonishment about patience or silence. With her left hand she tucked a flannel shirt into her snug denims, while a sawed-off shotgun swung in her right. Puffs of vapor trailed back from her face. An enlarging cloud of truck exhaust crept through the gate to meet her.

Kim propped the tip of the stubby shotgun on a wooden cross-beam in the gate, careful of the electrified metal. It was a pose calculated to be authoritative but not threatening—until necessary.

"IDs, boys," she shouted. "Step down here—badges and IDs. State yer business."

The truck doors fell open and two jumpsuited men strode to the gate. Each wore the yellow rectangle of Inspectors and produced cards from their hip pockets. They hadn't shaved in days. The smaller of the two, dark-haired, had one continuous eyebrow—no break at the top of his nose. His companion, a muscler, wore thick glasses that distorted the look of his face.

"We're Government," the first said, holding the card higher.

"I see dat."

"This is Faiging, right? We were routed in for an unscheduled stop—since we had open cargo space. Anything for Transport going northwest we can take. This'll count for next month's inspection, too. It's part of the efficiency program."

"Ficiency." Kim contemplated the word, in no hurry. "Fish-in-sea. I ain't been fishin' for weeks."

One-Eyebrow laughed, seemed friendly now. "Come on, let us warm up. You can check inventory." He poked a finger tentatively at a strand of wire weaving through the gate.

"Hey!" Kim screamed. One-Eyebrow stopped, surprised.

Kim stepped back and let the shotgun fall to her side. "You know how many wild dogs I gotta clean off'n this fence every mornin'? Shoot."

"I *know* it's electric. Just wondered how powerful."

"You wanna check an electric fence," she said, exasperated, "you don't do it with an open hand. Electricity makes ya muscles contract—you'll end up grabbin' a hot one till you're cooked through, boy. You touch a hot wire with the *back* of yer hand—that's how ya do it. That way yer hand closes *away* from the wire. Shoot."

One-Eyebrow nodded thankfully and tapped the back of his fingers on the wire. There was a flash, and a crackling like an overheated griddle slapped with fresh sausage. The Inspector recoiled, and lines of singed flesh gleamed red across each finger. His friendliness had evaporated.

Kim giggled and seemed for a moment almost effeminate. She fit a key into a centerpost of the gate, pulled up the ground bolts, and slid a cross brace aside. She pointed with the shotgun. "Garage number two, gentlemen. Please close the doors after ya—the outdoors is a bit much to heat this time a day. Meet ya at the house."

The pock-faced inventor was fussing over a plank with forty-eight small holes drilled into its face—four rows of twelve. Wires trailed from each hole, ending in a tiny horseshoe clip—electrical connections to be completed some other day. Set into the top of each hole was a light coil spring, and Faiging was placing buttons (sawed pieces of dowel) on top of each of them. Soon the contraption would be a crude electric keyboard.

Kim kicked through the spring door to the lab, and the two strangers followed. "Inspectors," she announced in a formal tone. "IDs are proper. Say they can pick up Transport shipments if we're ready. They been frisked."

Cred Faiging dropped a peg into its hole, consulted his diagram, then picked up his ink brush to paint the proper letter on its top—*H*. He regarded the newcomers.

"Unusual," he said.

The shorter of the two Inspectors was rubbing his right hand. "Unusual. Huh? Whatcha mean?"

"I see clearly that you are Inspectors—yellow badges, humph. We see Inspectors alla time. Got to, if we're gonna do business, no? Ya say ya can do Transport duty. Unusual . . ." Faiging selected another peg, placed it in a hole, and painted a letter—*J*.

"Efficient," said the shorter man, the one with the continuous eyebrow.

"My point exactly," said Faiging, returning his brush to its bottle and standing erect for the first time. He faced the men. "It would be quite efficient to allow Inspection service trucks to perform Transport duties, especially when you had vehicles up the mountains, this far from any city. My point precisely, fellows. I thought of that long ago—had suggested it to many Inspectors and Transporters. Efficient, yes. But Government, no. They don't go for it." He sighed. "I don't enjoy deceit—please tell me why you have really come."

One-Eyebrow consulted his wristwatch, exchanged glances with his cohort, and they both nodded. "You are right, Mr. Faiging, that we are not here to pick up shipment," he said. He poked a burned thumb toward Kim. "You will please ask your guard to give us her guns and ammunition. We had fifteen armed men in the back of each truck—tommies, hand bombs, nice Faigings, you'd wanna know. And as we speak they are taking control of the compound."

Faiging stared at his feet, and he looked weary, old. His lungs were emptying through his nostrils in a slow, steady hiss. When the sound stopped, his chest heaved again, and he asked, "Will you allow me a short speech?"

One-Eyebrow nodded, and his companion did the same, his thick lenses cutting visual swaths out of the sides of his face.

"I ask you to think apart from the Government for a moment," the inventor said. "Take that part of you which is the Government and set it here on the table, away from your human reason." This drew blank stares.

"Umm. How to say this? The Government needs me, for one thing. My production, my invention, they must be ongoing."

This time the tall one, the muscler with the glasses, responded. "None of that is our concern. The Monitor himself wants you."

"For what?"

"He said to tell you this, and that you would understand:

He has a large Bullet, an ancient one that stands upright in the ground. He wants to be absolutely sure it will fly—a final check before he fires it. You, with your electrical genius. You will come with us, or you will die. We will pack into the trucks any equipment that you need."

"I have heard of these Bullets," Faiging said. He was staring again at the floor. "But a final time: Is there room in your mind for anything but the Government? Anything but the *Monitor*? You can even live here if you like—there is warmth and food and sex and—"

The sentence was broken by two peals of laughter. One-Eyebrow and his sidekick pushed out the door and motioned for Faiging and Kim to follow.

32
The Chess Game

Anton Takk hadn't made a move in twenty minutes, and much to his irritation, Pec-Pec maintained a constant conversation as they pored over the chessboard.

Takk's more forward knight was trapped in an impossible crossfire. It could move nowhere, not even retreat, without being snared in Pec-Pec's clever web. And once that horseman fell, Takk knew, his defenses would steadily crumble. There was no way to save the knight, he was sure, unless he could find an ingenious diversion—a side skirmish that might eventually change the tenor of the game.

". . . and I certainly can understand why you are having trouble reconciling the concepts, but you have no reason to fear the Rafer man," Pec-Pec was saying. His braids, a few of them gold-tipped, hooded his face as his eyes danced over the chessboard.

"Just as you and I and Webb and the llamas and Gregory and the Inspector have been indispensable to our mission, Tha'Enton is playing an integral part as well. Daily he swags through an edge of existence that you will never see. He seems dangerous, and often he is. But the Rafers are my

141

children, and I think they will not harm anyone, especially while we are interdependent for our task.''

Takk glanced up wearily and looked down again. A pawn, perhaps, he was thinking. Advancing the queen bishop's pawn could well establish a protective base from which to launch a diversionary attack. If only the fatal onslaught would not come in Pec-Pec's next move. . . .

The two had stationed themselves on a rocky clearing with a panoramic mountain view. Pec-Pec had produced the chess set from his leather backpack, an astoundingly small container for all of the objects it seemed to carry. It was an intricately carved set of chessmen done in ebony and beech, and the comfortably worn board was a mosaic of the same woods. The pieces felt familiar to the touch, like old friends, and were weightless between the fingers as they were moved to each new position, as if they were quite aware of their assigned tasks. As the tension of the game mounted, they felt warmer.

If Takk found the conversation irritating, Pec-Pec had a distraction of his own. His eyes habitually wandered to a canyon in the western distance. Its walls were reddish rock, perhaps painted more red than usual by the falling sun. There was a scattering of scrubby trees, which grew thicker and larger at the rims of the canyon, and the narrow lake at its bottom was a sheet of blue glass. Pec-Pec was experiencing a new emotion: dread. He reached into his backpack, bunched several sunflower seeds into his fingers, and popped them into his mouth.

"Rosenthal Webb is over his fury now," Takk murmured. "We spoke this morning. Even asked how my lip was healing."

"Ah, yes."

"He tells me," said Takk, taking on an accusing tone, "that he gullies not this new land, but knowledge of it comes to him as if by magic. He says foreign ideas jump into his head out of nowhere—people to contact, direction of travel, that sort of thing. He says some new bugger has taken residence in his heart, a new kind of compass, one with no north or south. A dream compass vaning him across unknown territory.''

Pec-Pec looked up at him with wide-open eyes, inviting Takk to continue.

"I did not have to ask who this was—what person could possibly enter another man's mind, suggest that he do things he might not normally . . ."

"Ah," said the magic man. "Well. I am thinking that you deserve to know some of these things. Of course—you are not here merely by your own choice. Not you, or the others. You have been lured and dangled for things more important, yes. Yet this also is the world as it is, and you are playing your part in it, the only part you can possibly have. Stop and think: What man, really, can look down at his boots and say they are standing precisely where he wants them to be? Hmm?

"You worry about a few friends in trouble, you have small and private motives; I have a foreknowing—the purpose here is the undoing of a large evil. But we are making danger—there are no guarantees. Any of us could die."

Webb appeared on the outcropping. He was bare chested, showing the silvery pink scars mottling his right forearm and chest. The gray revolutionary sullenly lifted field glasses to his eyes with both hands.

"Hoy, Webb," Takk cried, "how does she look? Has Tha'Enton returned from the scout run?"

Webb lowered his glasses slowly. His eyes were rimmed in red, and his face, covered in ragged new beard, looked tired.

"Ya. The Rafer is back from running the canyon rims." The old revolutionary somberly limped off of the outcropping, and when he returned he was hefting one of the cartons that had been stacked near the llama hitch. He threw the case to the ground, a rough handling that made Takk twitch.

The revolutionary tore the top open and pulled out a six-inch steel cylinder. "This is the charge," he said. "The blaster seal—I keep those in a separate carton—ya fit over one end. Then"—he rapped on the side of the hand bomb—"any hard impact will set her off. Dynamite."

"Couple hunnerd of those," Takk said cheerfully, "would clear any canyon, ya?"

Webb was looking even older. "No. They're useless."

"What!" Takk was on his feet. "We hauled 'em a week across the mountains!"

"And afore that," Webb noted, "*I* hauled 'em across the continent. But Tha'Enton has done a thorough scouting, and we have a problem. *If* the Monitor is in the canyon, there's no way to tell where—not a structure to be seen, nothing to hit with a banger."

"No buildings? It must be the wrong canyon," Takk said. "Is the 'dream compass' a little off, ey?"

"It's the right canyon. There's a turbine, protected by a net, under a waterfall. She's got to be turning electricity, which means humans are about down there somewhere."

"We'll blow the turbine then."

"That might help, but it'd be a minor damage. And with that done, the bird people would hack us to spaghetti sauce. The birders, they're the guards what can fly, half a hunnerd of 'em round top of the canyon, the Rafer says." Webb flipped the cylinder in his hand and caught it by the opposite end. "And with these pokers to attack with, well, ya'd have to score a direct hit on one of the fliers to do any good."

"Fliers," Takk said, "not humans, ya mean?"

"Yes. Humans. On wing."

"Rifles would have worked nicely."

"Mayhap. But then, how would I have known what we were walking into?"

Pec-Pec glared up at the two from the chessboard. "This banger talk makes my gut turn," the magic man said. "Those bangers, all bangers, are a rot." He waggled a finger toward the chessmen. "The game. Your move now, half an hour."

Takk returned to his side of the board, folding his legs in front of him. "We go north now, I guess?"

Pec-Pec sighed and Webb about-faced and stalked off toward camp. "You still are determined to follow your penis to Blue Hole. But I tell you, I have a foreknowin' that your Nora Londi is not there, she is down in that canyon where the fliers swarm."

"But the fliers—ya didn't foreknow them too good, did ya?"

"Hmmph. I will go down into the canyon myself tomorrow. Then we will see what next."

Takk examined the chessboard anew in the dimming light, then looked up to meet Pec-Pec's eyes. "I have just realized . . ." Takk said.

"Oh?"

"I can checkmate you in two moves," the Northlander said, scratching under his beard.

"Oh, that. I was hoping you wouldn't see."

33
Tea

Nothing.

The two Inspectors stood perplexed in the empty compound outside Cred Faiging's lab house. They huffed short-lived little vapor clouds into the morning air and strode nervously into the clay yard.

There was supposed to be a battalion of Government men dispersed across the installation. Machine guns, grenades. The factories and lab surrounded. Garage No. 2, nearer the fence, stood silent and closed.

Kim pushed through the door and down the steps, Faiging lingering behind. "Sorry, fellas," she said grinning. "Guess I messed up. I'd heard a noise in the back of one of yer trucks. Figured it to be a rat or somethin', so I had the whole garage gassed with the trucks in 'er. Best way to exterminate—most thorough."

The shorter of the two Inspectors, the one with one continuous eyebrow, turned to confront her.

"You knew we were coming," he said, his outrage welling up. "You expected us *and killed thirty men!*"

Kim was swinging her sawed-off shotgun at her right

side. "An' I guess you guys was really gonna serve us tea and cookies, right? Is that what the orders mean when they say 'Eliminate all surplus personnel'? Dat mean pin bibs on us an' serve tea?"

The taller Inspector adjusted his thick glasses, hands starting to tremble. "What . . . where did you ever hear . . . something like that?"

Faiging had his arms crossed, a hand in each armpit to keep them warm. In a short jab, he pointed to the lab roof and tucked the hand back in. Perched above them was an odd electrical structure, looking like a giant wire mesh teacup, several feet across.

"Satellite dish," the inventor said, shivering now. He sounded like a child proud of an exquisite toy. "Had it for years. Printer hidden in the lab copies out any of the Monitor's dispatches. You gully satellites?"

"They'll figure it out," said One-Eyebrow, gaping upward. "They'll know what you've done."

"Oh, I dunno," Faiging said. "We can truck everything down the road a hunnerd miles, blow it up. Look like the revolutionaries done it. I'm making a new keyboard now, can send out some kinda message. I dunno yet. Somethin'."
He was backing up now.

Kim was still swinging the shotgun, and her brow pinched into an exasperated expression. "Both ya'lls flies are hanging open!"

When the two Inspectors looked down, she pulled off two rapid shots. She didn't have to look into their eyes.

Faiging forced himself to look at the steaming wounds. His ears were ringing like high-pitched sirens. "Kim, you're so dramatic."

"We done it, Boss. You ain't happy?"

"We bought a little time, is all."

34
Memoir

It was this night we started the Plan, and this small army I have shouldered into the Great Mountains is bedding weary. But it feels quite balls-out, and I laugh now—hunkering on this ridgetop a short shot from the center of Government, our scouts say, and preparing attack. And writing, *as I have done since childhood*, but writing without fear.

Hak! I am a tourist in my own life. All past is a closed book thrown on the fire. Tomorrow, perhaps all we have of the future, I cannot write yet.

In the day, this is the brightest place ever seen—we are so much closer to the sun, I suppose, so up these rocks. It is a happy blindliness, making battle and death seem quite impossible.

A qualmy commander would turn back now, considering what an odd root bag our forces make. How the old man Rosenthal Webb limped out this far, I dunno. His sidekick Gregory is a bright enough muscler, and he calls the gray-head sometimes Old Man Windmill, which Gregory swears has nothing to do with farting. There's a Rafer with us, out

*adark swinging in the trees now, I suppose. He develops a
fondness for Webb's mind, for Pec-Pec's mind, and the
flesh of all others—and I swear that I mean that not sexual.*

*Pec-Pec is quite a salamander. He tells an odd story on
being the father of all Rafers, and his father being some
kind of god to them. So you can see why he's not one to
try to gully to the bottom, lest you end up with a headache.
I like to think of such mouthings as balderdash, but you
cannot be sure with Pec-Pec. I have seen directly that the
man takes license with reality, with physical things.*

*And speaking of odd things, I have further observations
about the llamas, those beasts that we made hire of, the
ones that can talk, in our tongue, clear as mountain sky.
They haven't a memory, I have noticed—they never gully
much from days back. But they do think and talk. They do
talk.*

*I say to one llama, Salvadore, "With so little memory,
how do you know who you are one day to the next?"*

*And he stutters something like, "We live in packs. We
talk around what we know . . . keep collective knowing float-
ing among us. If one llama takes a roguish mind, the rest
of us can conspire to take care what he hears—edit his
memory—until his mind is right again."*

*That, of course, is leaving out all of Salvadore's hooms
and grunts and spits. Took him an hour to get that much
clear. But I put back to him, "What if once the single llama
is right and the many are wrong?" And he replies, "That's
never happened*—not that any of us can remember."

*And then it was that I decided to script some more, even
not knowing what I would do with this. That's what writing
is, I say: a permanent memory. No wonder the Government,
whatever that is, doesn't like it.*

*Our band is a mite hang-faced at my decision to leave
the hand bombs behind. But I insist they will not work here.
We must draw out the enemy, lure him with our vulnera-
bility. The bombs would only reach a soldier or two, not
the beast we seek.*

*Even the half-witted Inspector feels the tension. We
gagged him today to keep him from scream-singing into the
canyons for the pleasure of the echoes.*

For now, our task is reconnaissance. Pec-Pec says he is exploring the valley yonder in his mind-float, a buggabee that I will never understand. The Rafer Tha'Enton (if his ankle is not too swollen—I say there's bad damage, and he ignores it) will continue to run the canyon rim to scout upper lookouts and defenses.

We are hoping that the stronghold has depended mostly on its remoteness for defense—which is a factor we have only been able to conquer with the muscle of llamas and Pec-Pec's astounding mental reach, however it works, to steer us in the right direction. If there are legions defending the canyon, we will die. But if the Government has such forces in this wilderness, they might be of more regular use at the northward prison mine, Blue Hole, to be called down here only for some nasty bellyganger.

Well, we move in the next couple of days, and that's good, because my boots are shredding and I could use a bath. That flat lake, I can feel it now.

—Commander Anton Takk

Okay, I could not sleep. I wrote another lie: I am really the commander of nothing, and I put it down here on the worry that Webb might read this someday and hammer my lip again.

35
The Diary

When Nora Londi entered the massive dim room housing the thinker boxes, Loo and the llama Diego were working at the semicircular console in the center. The cool dryness was beginning to gnaw at her bones. It may be good for the machines, she thought to herself, but this ain't fit for humans—the Monitor, maybe, but not humans.

She folded her arms across her chest and waited for her eyes to adjust to the dark. She found the structure of the cavern and the labyrinth of rooms and passageways confounding. The Monitor claimed that the ancients had carved them out of the solid rock, but that was preposterous. Still, the interior seemed humanly deliberate sometimes, nothing like the haphazard river caves she knew from eastward. But the farther west you go, Londi thought, the less things make sense.

As she paced down a passageway, amid the humming thinker boxes and their odd acrid odor, Londi found her eyes drawn to the ceiling. It was dark, and the ceiling was high, but there appeared to be a gridwork of girders doming the room.

Loo's fingers were clattering over a keyboard on the counter, and she and Diego were exchanging an incomprehensible babble in that language that was tailor-made for the tongueless little woman. The screen glowed green as script moved across it. Londi decided not to speak, wondering if these passive machines could really hurtle the giant Bullet into the air, wondering what the words on the screen meant. Londi could not remember having wanted to read before.

And she had never known quite this sense of helplessness and despair, for the Monitor had put it to her quite bluntly: She was to become one of his breeding machines, a star player in his human kennel, with proceedings to begin the next day. Booger, is that what the village down by the beach was? A breeding pen?

Her eyes fell to Loo's forearms, which shone green in the machine's light like some velvety fabric. Londi wanted to touch the dark skin. She wondered if Loo had ever borne a child.

Loo rapped the llama on the snout, apparently a signal for him to stop talking. Diego recoiled with a scraping of hooves but obeyed. Shoving the keyboard aside, Loo pulled down a bulb-shaped microphone on its bendable stand. She spoke into it, "Hoo-ooooma. Oonga-hoor..." And the writing continued to spill across the screen, faster than ever. She pointed the microphone at Diego, who added his own words. When the script continued, the llama snorted gleefully at his contribution.

Diego turned, noticing Londi for the first time. "Oh, hooma, hello."

"Hello," she replied. "Learning to fly the sky machine? Or fire the big Bullet?"

Loo hooted a protest, and Diego answered, "No. She showing . . . diary in machine memory. Hoom."

"She'll still skin ya when the time's right."

Loo snarled and whirled around in her chair, firing a stream of knife-edged words. Diego translated cautiously: "Dooma, oom. She saying you . . . built backwards, too large, too—hoom—not smart. Cow in a cattle pen. . . ."

Londi was marching toward the passage to the outdoors,

her face aflame, and didn't hear the last of it. A succession of violent images paraded through her mind—a knife blade arcing through the air, a log chain whistling in a circle over her head, the crunch of a bone under her hands.

Her biceps tensed and eased with each memory.

She stopped at one of the thinker boxes and pounded its black metal hood. Loo and Diego had returned to their work and ignored the echoing crunch. An electrical cord ran from the back of the newly dented machine casing down to the floor, and Londi gave it a furious yank. It came free of the floor easily, the machine's lights died, and Londi studied the pronged plug at the cord's end. It looked like the bones of a severed wrist, she decided.

Outside, the sun was low in the west. Londi was surveying the cooling canyon spread before her when a peculiar, calming sensation crept through her body, slowly, from the base of her neck to her ankles, like the most powerful of barroom potions.

She glanced about the ledge and saw that she was alone. She loosed the leather tie holding her hair back and rubbed her scalp nervously with both hands. It was the feeling of swimming nude in a cold stream, and of being watched— maybe not exactly watched, but *with* someone, close, embracing, and even closer than that. Not carnal, but sexual nevertheless.

When panic rose in her chest, it subsided just as quickly, forcibly eased by this new presence. And then came the strangely accented voice in her head—*in her head*—resounding: *I am a friend, Nora Londi, do not be afraid. Your memory is now mine, too. Through you, I have seen the big Bullet. Thank you. I have seen the Bullet. Now let us examine the village.*

Londi stepped onto the rocky trail and carried Pec-Pec in her mind down the canyon wall.

36
Override

The crystals in the rock above the Monitor's oval bed began to glow faintly. His meaty white hand groped the bedside table until he found the mirrored sunglasses, and when he slipped them on, a relieved sigh gurgled up his throat. Outside, he knew, dawn was spilling into the canyon and seeping ever so dimly down the yards of rock corridor around several turns and into his chamber to burn at his sensitive eyes.

Uhhh.

Again his hand thumped across the table until he found the flask. He uncapped it with the flick of a thumb and turned it up against his lips. The thick syrup of distilled cactus oozed down his tongue, sour and sugary at the same time. He sat up with a grunt.

The Monitor had not slept well. A vague unease had kept his mind churning, searching for answers to the unanswerable. And he was beginning to admit that it was time to move headquarters—a notion that nudged him even closer to depression.

But there were immediate matters, too. He strode stiffly

to his desk and glared down at the printouts stacked on their open folder. The top dispatch was the source of his current distress:

> Code: A10–08 Yachette
> Destination: Monitor/Eyes only
> Routing: SATline/Scramble
> Origin: Pipbury Station wireless/Linex 64
> Message: Two Inspection vehicles on Monitor assignment destroyed in pass near Fontana. Thirty-two dead. Appears work of revolutionaries.

The Monitor had tried for two hours the day before to raise Pipbury Station, but the bumpkins seemed to have left their wireless unattended. He gulped again from his flask. His legs were warming now, his nerves snapping to life.

Something was amiss here. The revolutionaries had not even attempted such an attack for a dozen years or more. They seemed to have sagged into some sorry inertia, running such pathetic little missions that they were hardly worth persuing anymore. But as soon as the Monitor tried to have Cred Faiging picked up, the Security team was massacred. Cred Faiging, the genius of invention. The mechanical genius. The electronic genius.

The Monitor flicked on his computer terminal and squinted behind his sunglasses until his eyes adjusted to the light. He pecked in the code, destination, routing, and origin necessary to communicate with New Chicago Central Wireless—they would be in the office by now.

> Message: Trying to raise Pipbury Station. Please check status.

> Message: Pipbury Station in sporadic operation for last two months. Shipment of new receiver caroms is pending approval of capital purchase request.

> Message: Confirm Pipbury Station transmission to me at 17:00 yesterday your time, SATline/Scrambled routing, Code A10–08 "Yachette."

Message: Logs show no such transmission relayed
through New Chicago Central Wireless."

No such transmission? *All* transmissions, scrambled or otherwise, were relayed through Central Wireless. Unless someone had discovered how to tap into the satellite.

So. Cred Faiging was playing games—that was the best guess. Cred Faiging was not going to cooperate.

Cred Faiging would be dealt with later today. Then he would begin arrangements to move headquarters. But now . . .

The Monitor punched two buttons, and a record of his communication with Central Wireless clattered out of the printer. Then he cleared the computer screen and called up a program titled "Warhead Delivery Systems Launch Sequence."

He smiled, and a teardrop of saliva formed at the left corner of his mouth. There were only two parameter blanks left in the program, and he filled them in:

Diagnostic status: Override.
Launch timer: 1 hour.

An hour. Mmm. Time enough to hop down to the beach and watch the bullet soar.

He stored the program and imagined the wave of orders gushing into the Bullet—all the minutiae of trajectory, multiple warhead deployment, timing.

"Take that, Europe," he murmured at the blank screen.

He heard a distant rumbling, and he turned an ear toward the door. Not his Bullet, certainly not this soon. The noise was rhythmic, oddly lyrical. It sounded like music.

37
The Symphony

When Tha'Enton descended onto the beach he spat on his hands and rubbed them in the sand, hoping the sticky, browning bloodstains on his skin would scour away. One lookout on the north rim of the canyon would not be causing trouble when the sun came up this morning. But blood-sticky fingers would not do for a musician's virtuoso performance.

Every motion seemed painfully, epically more difficult than it needed to be. His ankle throbbed, and his mind was blistered with the demands of honor.

The llama Pinta, who did not speak any tongue that the Defender was familiar with, had handled the excruciating climb down the cliff in expert silence. He admired the beast. But now she seemed restless, and the hundreds of ebony sticks suspended in the frame strapped to her back tinkled with her nervousness.

He laid a hand on the Pa as it wobbled over the llama's shoulders, partly for support and partly to quiet the instrument. The Defender pointed gruffly to the black stretch of silent lake, and Pinta obediently began the mushy trek across the 100 yards of sand. It was a soothing walk, relatively, for the bearded warrior's damaged ankle—quite a relief from the stony mountainside. It is only pain, he told himself, just a feeling, something like tasting a sour fruit. Tha'Enton found himself thinking of the sea of pillows blanketing one of the Tan-Tan tents, and the Pleasure-Givers, and the incense . . . and then he forced his mind away from the homeland.

A narrow strip of sky along the eastern horizon had turned turquoise. Instinctively, Tha'Enton searched the still-black dome above for the Orion constellation, and when he found the Hunter's three-star belt, he murmured the Defender's prayer, one line for each star:

"Honor the enemy with death,
Honor the weapon with a sure toss and a warm home,
Honor the body with bravery."

The air whispered faintly of sea life, reminding him of the Southland marshes. At the edge of the wet sand, Tha'Enton set up the Pa. The lake edge rustled with minuscule wave action, and the Defender-Sounder decided that would be the First Sound, the foundation on which the coming musical composition would be built.

He had purposely descended the canyon wall just west of the cliff-side village. He positioned the Pa so that he faced east, the view taking in the cluster of mud and rock homes just above the sand, the cliff trails, the long finger of beach and the distant waterfall gushing into the turbine. Tha'Enton heaved his weight onto each of the Pa's three legs until they were firmly planted in the hard undersand. Then he began the tedious task of unclamping each set of 718 bones so that they teetered freely on the quarter-sphere rack, ready to be twittered between the musician's fingers.

That done, the musician untied his waist-skin and tucked it under one of Pinta's backstraps. Naked and ready. His only adornments, ironically, were functions of fighting: the quiver over his shoulder, a knife strapped to each calf, and a burnished brass crotchplate. If his will not to draw blood was to be tested—tempted—then it should be a real test, he reasoned, with all of the tools of war at hand.

Either he would be warmed soon by the sun or he would be dead; whichever, he would have no need for skins. The Defender swatted Pinta on the rump and shoved her toward the cover of the boulders at the far side of the beach.

Of course, the music started with nature, the reproving click-click of the lake waves. The waterfall layered on a cool, seamless hoosh, and a family of desert toads somewhere was awakening to the growing light with *cree-dit, cree-dit, cree-dit*. Tha'Enton began his contribution with the most subtle of low tones, rattling imperceptibly the thickest, longest Pa sticks along the bottom row of the rack.

The symphony was ten minutes old before anyone seemed to notice. A man appeared on the sand with a toddler in tow. They approached cautiously, mouths agape. Both were naked, deeply and evenly tanned, and both had prodigious bellies that waddled as they crept forward. They were dark, yet their features were obviously those of the Fungus People, Tha'Enton decided.

He felt his chest ease with relief: Could these sorry specimens be the sort of beings running such a putrid and murderous Government? It takes no kind of warrior to pull the trigger of a gun, or to throw the hand bombs. . . . And then he banished the thought, for he had to concentrate on the music. All else would fall in place—it was the word of Pec-Pec, son of Rutherford Cross, and that was all he needed to know. Music was all that was required of Tha'Enton today, orchestrating a stunning musical piece, and he must not sway from that duty. He began to blend in a slightly higher toned row of bones.

The Fungus Man squatted on the beach, puzzled and enthralled, his scrotum a defeated balloon sagging onto the wet sand. His son mimicked the posture, ill equipped for the latter effect, and both gawked innocently, unaware of Tha'Enton's working title: *Song of Cataclysm*.

The sky brightened and more villagers appeared out of the rising mist. The Sounder's hands danced across the instrument, his Pa tones rose, and the rhythms grew confoundingly complex.

In the corner of Tha'Enton's vision there appeared a tiny

pair of wings far above at the canyon rim. Then another, and yet another, until the newly blue sky was aswarm with distant bird people, slowly circling, descending. In the morning light, Tha'Enton began to sweat.

A shrill cry echoed down from the milling flock, apparently the leader, sounding like an enraged bayou egret: *Kaioonga, oom, kaim-oon*. And the Sounder harumphed at such an addition to his orchestration. The falling swarm reminded him of being hit by a Flinger's weighted hunting net, but again he dispensed of the thought quickly.

When the music rose to crashing waves of sound, with Tha'Enton flinging showers of sweat from his soggy braids and beard, a figure appeared at the mouth of a cave high up the canyon wall. The muscley, porcelain white body writhed in a spasm of exertion; seconds later arrived the sound of the snarling bellow he had heaved down the slope.

The villagers watching the performance gasped and gurgled in unison and fanned out frantically across the sand toward their homes, lest they draw the Monitor's wrath. The bull monster started his tedious descent, an astonishing combination of sprints, frog leaps, and skittery slides down gravel banks.

A half hour later, just short of the beach, the Monitor halted on top of one of the adobe huts and appeared to be shuffling gear about and hollering down into the house. A large llama appeared through the hatchway, and then a large woman, both having a painful time adjusting to the light. The Monitor furiously lashed Nora Londi's hands behind her back and shoved her off the mud hut. She hit the beach hard and awkwardly, belly first—"Hoo!"—and squirmed to free her face from the sand. Anticipating similar treatment, the llama Diego dived from the rooftop—a dangerous fall, but better done under one's own control. He landed on the beach with a graceful running motion and a shock-absorbing bending at the knees.

The Monitor thudded into the sand just beside them, and after a series of kicks and howled threats, the two captives reluctantly trudged in the direction of the strange, but not displeasing, music. Londi, dazed, leaned heavily into the llama for support.

The Monitor seemed maniacally incensed at the foreign musician's intrusion, while the reason for fury escaped Londi and Diego. The man-beast shouted into the sky, gurgling with frothing phlegm: "Loo! All of you! Grab that pig-poking Rafer, and watch his quiver. De-ball him, and hold him for me!"

The bird people hummed close, and en mass they tilted their wings for a menacing dive toward the beach's edge. Tha'Enton studied the change in trajectory with trepidation. He knew the dreadful weapons these airborne beasts carried—he had just killed one of them on the canyon rim—but his assignment, from the highest of gods save Rutherford Cross himself, was that he must continue the music. He would not lift a weapon. He would not waver from the soundings, and he forced himself to consider how next he might flavor the symphony.

At that moment the decision was made for him. A long black form catapulted out of the white rush of waterfall. It arced into the air like an arrow and, halfway down to the sheet of blue lake, the sticklike shape stopped in midair and bounced—snagged by the expansive hemp web protecting the turbine. Tha'Enton smiled: His companions beyond the waterfall were indeed doing their part, and the anguish of loneliness began to dissipate.

Then began a new chapter of musical history, with Tha'Enton the conductor. The murderous bird people were at killer tilt, seconds away; the Monitor himself was just a few dozen wrathful strides down the beach. And a second tree trunk rocketed off the waterfall, swan-dived into the net, and . . . *booooooooooong*.

The sound of the two logs crashing thundered down the canyon, then spilled over onto its own echoes. Even the Monitor stopped mid-beach; it was the exquisite, undeniably perfect underlayering for Tha'Enton's musical work. The Rafer flushed, and his crotchplate bulged outward. It was the lowest of low tones, the chiming of a Pa so large that only a god could hope to manage such a contraption.

A third tree trunk split the air at the far end of the canyon, and its crash into the net was the perfect complement to the dying tone just rung by its predecessors. Tha'Enton shivered, but did not break stride with his own part of the music.

The fourth, fifth, and sixth logs also crashed into the net with perfect timing, and finally the mirror-eyed Monitor, stalled on the sand, reassessed his orders. The gnarled muscles of his snouted countenance fell into a sag as he regarded the mounting pile of logs in the net over the turbine—a net grown taught, a net becoming dangerously stressed.

And then he screamed new orders to his legions falling from the sky: "The net! Get those logs *out of the net!*"

Thundering voice. Booming tree trunks. The bird people peeled away toward the far end of the canyon, and the Sounder's grin bared two rows of dingy, sharpened teeth. His symphony was coming along splendidly. It was a symphony to die for.

38
Logging

Gregory removed his shirt and tied it awkwardly across his mouth to filter out the sawdust. His was a broad, fleshy chest, a girth the young revolutionary was rather proud of—a pride that withered when the Northland dullard Anton Takk stripped his torso as well. The odd bearded man, who took such pride in his limited reading and writing abilities, seemed oblivious to his physical attributes—that remarkable warehouseman's build.

Takk's mouth twitched impatiently at Gregory's stare, and the former log-camp worker motioned him back to the two-man saw.

"Can't fall behind," Takk said. "It'll ruin it all." Two dozen trimmed tree trunks made an orderly stack at the riverside.

"We should have done this yesterday," Gregory complained, leaning into the broad blade, pleased at least that his makeshift mask was saving his lungs from further dusting.

"Couldn't a done it without drawing the attention of those cave creepers down there," Takk said, nodding downstream. "I gully they're a might distracted nowabouts. The surprise is best."

"You seem to have a lot of faith in this foolishness. My way, I'd haul down the hand bombs. By now, the cannibals, they've put the Rafer to a roasting spit."

Takk didn't answer. How to combat the lethal bird people with hand bombs—the lithe little killer beasts that Tha'Enton and Pec-Pec described—was beyond him.

It was a bit late, Takk thought, for Gregory to become a fan of Rosenthal Webb's hardware. Pec-Pec called the bangers spiritually abhorrent; now Takk was also glad they had been left at the old camp, up on the mountaintop. Pec-Pec had returned from a mind-float insisting again that Nora Londi was in the canyon, not at Blue Hole. Who knows— aimless bomb tossing could kill her, and that would be the ender for Takk. He would drown himself.

Down the bank, Webb worked with the llamas. They had found the ferry rigging across the river intact, although little was left of the dory itself. Webb had assumed that someone had played a bit of sabotage against Government Transport, until Pec-Pec awakened with his odd tale about Nora Londi shattering the little boat.

It was the llama Salvadore who devised the method for getting the logs into the strong center current. Two llamas labored on each side of the bank. They were loosely yoked (as they refused to be actually tied to the rigging), and their lines were knotted to the O-rings that had drawn the old dory across the river.

Webb had fashioned a rope cradle suspended from the O-rings. As he sat in that web the llamas could draw him in and out of the river, as if he were a pair of trousers on a pulleyed clothesline. Salvadore stood on the bank, rubbery lips pursed, staring at the pocket watch Webb had placed among the stones. With Webb harnessed midstream, holding a newly felled tree trunk in the numbing current, Salvadore would raise his head, dignified, calling out at forty-three-second intervals: "Now!"

(The night before, Gregory had fomented a great row about this timing business. Pec-Pec had feigned surprise at the outburst and held court for a half hour on the interlockings of art, religion, nature, strategy, and fate. Finally, Webb had just ordered Gregory to shut up.)

Webb released a log, it arrowed downstream, and the yoked llamas hauled Webb out of the stream to get another. Slapping his arms, Webb scrambled for the tree pile, harness lines trailing. "Couldn't someone start a little fire for me?" he complained.

Salvadore glanced down at his hoofs and up again, perplexed. The only unoccupied human was the mindless Inspector Kerbaugh, equally incapable of supplying a warming blaze.

They had considered lashing Kerbaugh to a tree while the others worked, to keep him from wandering into the forest. But an unexpected object near the ferry landing served as babysitter. Kerbaugh squatted in his filthy tunic, held rapt by a human head atop a three-foot stake. It was red-bearded and aswarm with flies.

Pec-Pec sat cross-legged nearby, eyes closed, an empty fishbowl in his lap.

39
The Man in the Hat

My name's Mickey Kerbaugh. My Auntie Mommie made up a song about the Man in the Hat. It goes:

> *He'll tear your hair*
> *And bite your nose.*
> *He'd like to chop*
> *Your trouser hose!*

Auntie Mommie used to tell me to stay in bed or the Man in the Hat would come get me like he came got Mommie. Auntie Mommie would *do* each line as she sang it. You know, I'd be under the covers, and she'd grab my hair and pull my head back for the first part and it hurt. Then she'd pinch my nose. And then, well you know, she'd punch me . . . down *there*.

Auntie Mommie is not real Mommie, because the Man in the Hat came got real Mommie when she turned red. I *said* that. Then I went to live with Auntie Mommie. And later Auntie Mommie turned red too, and the Man in the Hat came got her. Finally I left Nawlins and nobody ever is allowed to go back there. Nobody. Or maybe they'd turn red too. I didn't, but maybe *they* would.

The Man in the Hat wears long black clothes. He has a long beard and brown teeth and smells like pee-pee. He even gave me black candy when Mommie turned red, and it tasted like worms. He watches at night from the black outside the window, and he'll come get me next. Auntie Mommie said so.

Well, I'm with the Big People now, and today I found a new friend. He lives by the water near the little fish and his name is Mr. Funny Nose, and all of the Little Green People like him a lot.

I could sing a song but the Big People don't like it. Maybe I could sing a song for Mr. Funny Nose.

40
Losing Ground

The Monitor bellowed, flinging sweat, apoplectic with fury. The bird people obediently changed course for the endangered turbine and the sagging net full of logs. But it was evident to all observers on the beach that only one of the fliers—a particularly lithe winger—was recouping enough height to make a net landing.

Londi was baffled by the scenario, particularly the Rafer musician. But the destruction of the turbine—whoever was behind the scheme—had obvious appeal. Her wrists still firmly lashed behind her, her rib cage newly bruised from the fall to the beach, she swung painfully onto Diego's back and murmured "Go!" Either they would be immediately torn apart in the Monitor's hands, or they would quickly be out of his reach.

Diego snuffled in surprise, sprang away, and they were yards down the sand. The Monitor was still belching orders into the sky.

"Can you hold me?" shouted Londi, alarmed that the llama was staggering.

The llama cocked his head, but did not slacken the hoof

pounding: "If stay, hoom . . . to wet beach. Watch . . . balance."

Londi leaned forward and bit into Diego's neck wool for
support. She scanned the sky. "They're all going for the
net, not us," she mumbled through the fur. "Orders. But
we'll be in tomorrow's soup if this doesn't work."

"*You* soup. I be rug."

Londi worked at the bindings behind her back as Diego
galloped, his shoulders two bony pistons under her chin.
The leather tie on her wrists gave little, and Londi felt the
sting of sweat meeting blood. They pounded past several
frustrated bird people on the beach who had fallen short of
the turbine. Those fliers trotted east, wings folded on their
backs, perplexed by the passing sight of the giant woman
bouncing on top of a speeding llama.

Where the beach petered out and gave way to canyon
wall at the shadowed east end, Diego stopped. "Off," he
said flatly. "Can't carry up." His lungs wheezed and his
wool lay flat, sweaty.

As Londi dismounted a single bird woman alighted on
the net's main support above. It was Loo. The flier quickly
folded her wings and, spiderlike, she crept into the net.

Diego gave a puppylike whine. "Will you . . . must hurt
Loo?" he asked, watching the bird woman start to work.
Londi frowned but didn't answer.

The Rafer musician's thrumpings were drowned now in
the waterfall rumble, but Londi discovered that his rhythms
were still with her. She could feel precisely when the next
log would crash into the net—*there . . . ka-choong*.

There were more than a dozen logs in the net, and Loo
dashed for the newest arrival in what first seemed to be a
comic mismatch in weight. The bird woman used the log's
impetus to roll it part way up the net. She crouched under
the tree, adding her force to the roll, feet pumping from
one cross-rope to the next. Her progress slowed when the
log's fall force expired, but clearly she would make it to
the net's edge, where the log could be shoved into the lake
safely away from the turbine.

Londi hopped up from boulder to boulder, climbing the
canyon wall, hoping she would find a trail. The rocks were

perpetually damp from spray. Her feet slipped dangerously, and she stamped impatiently to free the wet beach sand from her boot treads. Just as Loo's first log splashed into the lake, another smacked into the net, its boom the only sound audible above the squalling waterfall. At best Loo would be able to prevent the log pile from increasing until help arrived. Londi looked down: A scattering of bird people were just minutes away.

Londi arrived, gasping, at the point where the net's northeast guy line was anchored to the rock wall. There, a steel post the width of her torso was cemented into the stone. The guy line was double braided at the end and looped over the post. Another log hit the net, and the post showed no strain. She knelt under the rope and shouldered upward, hoping to shove it off the post and collapse the net. Impossible. Too much weight and tension. She thought of rope-walking the 200 feet to the net, but the line was green with slime.

Bird people arrived at the beach's end below. Londi climbed higher, wishing she could use her hands as the slope steepened. Her knee joints ached.

Loo rolled another log into the lake. She was falling behind.

41
Samba in the Shallows

The Monitor stopped screaming when he saw the first log hit the lake with a white splash. He had sprinted down the beach himself until it appeared his minions would soon swarm the net and empty it safely. Now he wiped a rivulet of phlegm onto his forearm and turned back to regard the musician, who was mesmerized in his own frantic poundings. They were alone on the beach.

The monster grinned, his snout crinkling back. His skin was beginning to glow, both flushed with fury and starting to burn under the climbing sun.

It was fine music. The Monitor samba-stepped in its direction, his bare feet swishing in shallow water. It had been months since he had tasted Rafer meat.

The Sounder kept to the music, his faith pushing back intrusive mental pictures of each of his weapons.

42
Now

Loo's hands and forearms were awash with blood from a growing number of deep scratches. She had tried a short-cut—perhaps time could be saved by rolling the logs just halfway up the slope and sliding them through a hole in the netting. But the new method was too cumbersome and dangerous. Most of the logs had limb nubs that caught easily in the rope. And just one such snag could set a log swinging unpredictably, perhaps tossing it toward the turbine.

So Loo returned patiently to the earlier method. The logs stacked up. The ropes grew distressingly taut. Where were the other fliers? She tried crying out a warning, but it was useless against the water thunder.

When the net trembled once again, Loo expected the accompanying log blast, but there was none. She turned, afraid and puzzled: Had a support given way? If one guy line snapped, she guessed, the others would quickly follow. But the lines were in place, vibrating angrily, and the tower of white mist methodically pounded the mountain of tree trunks in the center of the net. She heaved one log over the net's rim as another crashed into place. Panting, Loo rope hopped wearily down the slope.

When she arrived at the log pile, the fierce, bulletlike shower quickly erased the blood from her forearms. The coating of blood would return again in the coming minutes, as it had with sickening regularity.

Loo stepped up the pile until she found a log that could be pulled away freely. She stepped deeper into the stinging shower to put an arm around one end and roll the log down, the pine bark biting into her wrist. A dark shadow flickered back in the blinding white mist. She put her other arm to her brow to ward off the gale, squinted, and suddenly found herself scissored between the legs of a falling giant.

They landed hard on the side of the log pile, Nora Londi on top of Loo. The bird woman heard her wings crunch under her back and a sickly moist pain stabbed at her right side.

Panicking, Loo clawed at the shattered wing wood under her. The knife. A knee rammed her jaw, and Loo's vision dimmed. The large woman was a crushing weight, and Loo's lungs could not expand enough to meet demand.

Nora Londi's hair streamed down in a wild mass of red seaweed. Her hands were still bound behind her, and she leaned down awkwardly to tear a chunk of wing from under her slender captive—the shard that held the flier's knife, a knife that would make quick work of the netting. Then the giant seemed becalmed. A slight smile pressed her cheeks back. The two women traded stares, and Londi leaned down as if to share a cosmic secret with her trembling companion. Londi's head bobbed rhythmically, her stair-stepped nose touching Loo's ear. Over the howl of thrashing water she shouted one word, *"Now!"* and rolled away into the white cloud. Loo lifted her head into the torrent, aching, puzzled, and then the log landed.

43
The Hallucination

Over the distant net, Tha'Enton saw a curious mushroom cloud of red mist rise around the waterfall and settle quietly into the lake. It was an omen, he knew, harkening back to ancient times.

The Monitor was dancing maliciously nearer, but the Sounder stuck to his duty, fingers picking through the field of Pa bones. Even when the reddening monster arrived, lungs gurgling, breath like soured garlic, Tha'Enton did not break stride. He could not.

And then a riotous metallic boom echoed up the canyon and back again. The Monitor turned to look; the musician played. There was no more net under the waterfall, no more pile of logs. No more turbine. Just two thick shafts angling down from the rock into the lake.

The Monitor stamped in the sand with both feet and a squeal rattled to the top of his throat. He turned back to Tha'Enton, slinging saliva onto the Pa.

Tha'Enton studied the sticky bones, deciding how he would proceed with the music. The Monitor swept a hand

down on the Pa, and it collapsed in a clatter like a child's
toy log building.

The Song of Cataclysm was over. The offended Sounder
trembled, rage and horror raking his body. But the Pa was
not repairable, and the music had become instantly irrele-
vant. His faculties regrouped toward the second of his Rafer
duties—finally, he reasoned, with the music done he could
become Defender.

Tha'Enton pictured his next move: His right foot would
step back, he would crouch slightly, drop both arms down
to the thigh straps, and whirl forward with both knives
drawn.

The Monitor thought quicker. Before the musician could
move, the bull-beast had kicked his heel into his gut, and
Tha'Enton collapsed on the beach, his airless lungs writhing. Mere breathing brought a scraping of broken ribs. A
gratuitous kick to the jaw jolted his brain into a starry blackness.

"Ah, stripping down one more Rafer. You don't need
these." Tha'Enton heard the words through his shrieking
pain. He felt his knives being unstrapped by deft fingers
and his quiver peeled away. *The beast is so huge,* a fright-
ened inner voice cried, and he fought to turn that notion
away. The warrior in him knew that girth was just one factor
and pain did not matter. Pain was just a message from body
to brain, a message of distress. Pain did . . . not . . . matter.

When his vision cleared, the Monitor was shaking the
arrows and thrower disks out of his quiver. The Monitor
tossed the quiver at Tha'Enton's face, then picked the disks
out of the sand, seeming to savor their historic Rafer in-
scriptions, and tossed them one at a time over the lake.
They skipped like smooth stones and disappeared.

"I have killed many Rafers," the Monitor said gleefully,
throwing another disk side-armed, "but not for such a long
time."

It seemed that death was gnawing at his chest like a large
rodent, and Tha'Enton set about a final set of stark observations: A smashed Pa, blasphemy to the art of music; sand
in his mouth, and blood bubbling up his throat and through
his teeth; the discarded quiver, inches from his nose, a finely

tooled leather tube that bulbed slightly near the bottom, where he had jammed an odd-sized . . . unmentionable object.

And to his own horror, that despicable mass of molded metal at the bottom of his quiver became a goal, an object that could wield some small influence on a darkening day. A gun. A device of astounding butchery against his tribe. Sickening weapon of the Fungus People.

Tha'Enton reached. Cracked ribs shifted and scraped like gravel. *Pain . . . does . . . not . . . matter.*

Near the bottom of the quiver his hand fitted around the evil mechanism, and nausea overlayered the torture of a crushed chest. He pulled weakly. The gun held fast.

The Monitor was watching now, amused, thinking he had emptied the quiver. Tha'Enton had never fired a pistol. Did he have to do more than pull the trigger—find a safety catch, perhaps? Didn't guns have a safety catch? Where? Could a bullet be accurately fired through hard leather? Was he dying dishonorably, waging final battle with a contemptible firearm?

He pulled again, and the gun would not come free of the quiver. The Defender lifted his arm, carrying the quiver with it. His midsection howled pain. Awkwardly, he tried to estimate the trajectory: from wavering gun barrel to Monitor's forehead.

Extreme pain can suspend sanity. Sometimes the result is blackout, sometimes hallucination.

As Tha'Enton attempted to aim at the Monitor's face, the world seemed to tilt out of logical balance. Nature went berserk—he had no other explanation for it.

From high above, over the distant rim of the canyon, came a hellish growl. The Monitor's smile broadened and he turned his reddened face to see. From this distance, Tha'Enton decided, it looked quite like a Bullet of the Fungus People. A collosal Bullet borne upward out of the rock on a column of flame, slowly edging skyward.

A small panel blasted away from the side of the Bullet, an explosion made noiseless under the howl of the engine. Sparks spewed from the hole, then a furious billow of smoke. The Bullet wavered, and then the entire shaft folded in half and collapsed back to earth.

The giant spash of fire obliterated the trees at the top of the canyon rim where bird people had once perched. Bits of spinning, flaming debris began their long arcing descent through the pure canyon air.

The Monitor crouched and snarled, his upper lip curling back from his teeth in surreal fury over the lost Bullet. Like a slavering boar, the beast crept forward on all fours, fixed upon the flesh of the musician's neck.

And then Tha'Enton saw the canyon lake come alive, a final rent in the fabric of reality. A dozen square yards of the lake's surface, once a mirror, now roiled with foam. A woman rose, spiritlike, from the white circle. She was pale skinned, dark red hair an unruly, sopping mane. A giantess. This was the sort of vision, Tha'Enton told himself, that the scriptures spoke of, a stunning power promised by Rutherford Cross himself.

In a lightning flash, the woman burst from the water, mounted atop a streaming rainbow of reds and golds. As she bounded into the sky, Tha'Enton saw more clearly: The woman was straddling an impossibly large fish, a water beast the thickness of three tree trunks, streamer fins flapping like battle banners. The magnificent, writhing dragon fish angrily plummeted to the beach. It bared a row of razor teeth and neatly nipped off the Monitor's head.

44
Last Words

Now what? The Government has no head.

Damned if I was going to try to haul such a huge corpse, head or no head, up the canyon to bury it. And the beach sand didn't dig but a few feet before we hit rock. The villagers, quite cooperative considering the mayhem we brought yesterday, supplied us with a dory to haul the body to centerlake, where they say it's hunnerds of feet down. Tied his ankles to a rock and splashed him in. I'll never know what his face really looked like.

The birders, while less than friendly, have agreed still to stand watch on the canyon rim. Them that have tongues aren't speaking too well of this Monitor bugger, nor his bloodsome little sidekick, Loo, who didn't fare much better when we attacked.

Rosenthal Webb has spent most of his life as a revolutionary, and I suppose has a lot of gully in how things ought to be run—although I 'spect now he'll find that sabotage is easier than making things right.

The way the Government has already been set up here, as Webb sees it, will be useful for a month. Webb's man

Gregory, a hillbunkin a little younger to me, has the most mind for this electronics business (claims to know Cred Faiging). He says there is a small bit of power storage, which might hold that long without the turbine.

The turbine's drubbing, Gregory 'spects, had something to do with the crash-down of the Monitor's Bullet. Or mayhaps not. We found papers that show the Monitor had been sending for Cred Faiging, needed him for some drastic reason. Could be the Bullet never was flight ready.

Whatever, I was surprised to be told that the firewhack we witnessed was nay but the Bullet's fuel expending. Had nothing to do with the atomic banger the ancients had arranged. That mechanism, I gully, is melted amid the wreckage up on the canyon rim, and we're to avoid the vicinity for a few hunnerd years. I can manage that.

The villagers aren't fiery about rebuilding the turbine, and don't seem to want to leave with us either. They have most everything: shelter, food, and water from the lake, little garden patches, year-round summer down this far. It's as if they've shrugged off an employer and are just as happy going independent.

"As long as the work's no harder...." one said.

A blase bunch.

It was fiercely talked, but we've decided not to announce the Monitor's death, not for now. The Government is being run smoothly by a llama named Diego, who learned the thinker boxes from the birder named Loo. Rather than scramble New Chicago into chaos, Webb and Diego have laid out a schedule of dismantling that will allow Webb's people and myself to set on the city and take reins. Then the llamas will return to the mountains. They aren't much for Governments or things human.

Inspector Kerbaugh we'll leave here. He likes wearing no clothes and chasing minnows in the shallows. I hope he learns to leave his wenus alone in public.

All of us—except Pec-Pec—were surprised that Tha'-Enton survived the Monitor's drubbing. Those two do have a knowing between them. The Rafer is hobbling sadly but won't admit to any pain. Webb says Tha'Enton insists he'll be travel-worthy when he and Gregory leave in a few days.

The Rafer is adamant about accompanying them back east. Odd. He was none too companionly on the way out here.

I'll be leaving about the same time, once I've browned my skin a little on the beach. But I will go north, to Blue Hole. Diego is wiring ahead special instructions about the protection and release of Ben Tiggle, if he still lives. Webb says he's tempted to just order the entire work camp freed, and may do that once he's studied the inmate roll.

And Nora Londi says she wants to spit every time she smells me. I'll try again once her fury subsides. She did let on that she'd be making her way back to New Chicago sometime after her baby is born.

Which is the oddest part of these doings: How can a woman know she's just a day or two pregnant by a man she has never met before? Pec-Pec pulled her from the lake yesterday after she cut the net and fell with the log pile. Everyone is telling this dragon fish tale that I still don't gully—a monster what was Pec-Pec really, but then again wasn't—ach. And there beside the Monitor's fresh corpse Pec-Pec says to her, "You are having my child." And Londi shook her soggy head yes. I am depressed. Pec-Pec said he did it while doing his mind-float, that he did it as a precaution—ha!—because of something the Monitor was planning. To breed, like a dog, he said.

Pec-Pec looked tired. Said something about having to leave the dragon fish alone for a while, that it was a wilder bugger than he had ever imagined.

Pec-Pec then left the canyon straight away, backpack strapped on—marched right up the rock wall. We'd look up every half hour or so, and his little black figure grew tinier and tinier until he topped the rim just before nightfall. The canyon rim glowed red, and blip he was gone.

I miss Pec-Pec already, and hope to see him again. He left us with these strange words: "Me, I'm gonna rest these ol' bones now."

THE CONTINUATION
OF THE FABULOUS
INCARNATIONS OF IMMORTALITY
SERIES

PIERS ANTHONY

FOR LOVE OF EVIL
75285-9/$4.95 US/$5.95 Can

Coming Soon
from Avon Books

AND ETERNITY
75286-7